WITHDRAWN
FROM COLLECTION

# A TEMPORARY ARRANGEMENT

Roz, a career-minded HR worker, and Sam, a successful country and western singer, are good friends. *Just good friends* — who have been engaged to each other for six years . . . Their sham attachment began by mutual agreement: a way of keeping the media from nosing into Sam's private life, and stopping Roz's Great-Aunt Ellen fretting about her great-niece's single state. And it's worked like a dream — until now. Because Roz wants to end the pretence. But Sam seems oddly reluctant to do so . . .

*Books by Pamela Fudge*
*in the Linford Romance Library:*

RELUCTANT FOR ROMANCE
ROMANTIC MELODY
LOVE AND LIES

PAMELA FUDGE

A TEMPORARY
ARRANGEMENT

*Complete and Unabridged*

LINFORD
*Leicester*

First published in Great Britain in 2015

First Linford Edition
published 2016

A catalogue record for this book is available
from the British Library.

ISBN 978–1–4448–3018–7

Published by
F. A. Thorpe (Publishing)
Anstey, Leicestershire

Set by Words & Graphics Ltd.
Anstey, Leicestershire
Printed and bound in Great Britain by
T. J. International Ltd., Padstow, Cornwall

This book is printed on acid-free paper

# Dedication

This novel is dedicated to the memory of my dear friend, Cecelia Nesbit.

# For Cecelia
# A Dear Friend

My friendship with Cecelia
Lasted over fifty years
Mostly filled with laughter
Or we dried each other's tears
I enjoyed her words of wisdom
Her funny turns of phrase
She was never one to criticise
Always generous with her praise
A whiz with a crochet hook
Celia really was the best
She made matinee coats and lacy tops
And my gorgeous wedding dress
A lady with a zest for life
She coped with all that came her way
But was always at her happiest
When family came to stay
Ninety-six amazing years
A long life at an end
There was no one quite like Celia
I was blessed to call her my friend

© Pam Fudge / 10 May 2015

# Acknowledgements

I am blessed every day to have the love and support of my lovely family, my children, Shane, Kelly, Scott, not forgetting Mike and Jess and my gorgeous grandchildren, Abbie, Emma, Tyler, Bailey, Mia and Lewis.

Also thanks to my sisters, Barb and Pat, my stepdaughter, Rachel, and my web-master and stepson, Mark who count among my regular readers as do my wonderful friends Pam M, Pam W, Karen, Chris N, Chris H, Nora, Sheila, Jan, Angela, Helen, Sally and Dex, and to Margaret and Maurice, Beverley and Anna who have always been so supportive.

Finally, I could never forget Eddie and Frank who shared my life through two great marriages and left me with the best of memories.

# 1

'What do you mean, 'no'? You agreed — *we* agreed — that we would call it a day the minute either of us wanted out of what was only ever supposed to be a temporary arrangement. Well, I *do* — and so the engagement is *off*, Sam Lawrence, whether you like it or not.'

Roz could hear her voice rising, an awful, shrill, shrew-like note creeping in. She stopped, forcing herself to get a grip on her rising temper and calm down. Screaming down the phone and getting into a childish slanging match clearly wasn't going to get her anywhere at all.

Why on earth Sam was being so unreasonable, Roz had absolutely no idea; but she made herself take a deep, steadying breath before she added, a little more evenly, 'You can't do this to me, Sam. You just can't.'

'Let's talk about it.' The deep voice was soothing and aggravatingly reasonable as he continued. 'Why not take a break and come down to Dorset?' His tone became coaxing. 'Then we can spend some time talking things through and looking for a compromise, I promise.'

Roz held the receiver at arm's length, glaring at it in patent disbelief and scowling horribly. She could feel her hackles rising again, along with the bristling red of her hair.

'We don't need to talk,' she hissed, the moment she found her voice again, 'or look for a compromise. There is absolutely nothing to talk about, and I have no intention at all of coming down to Dorset. I'm far too busy.'

She had meant it at the time, but Roz wasn't totally surprised when she found herself boarding a South West Train at Waterloo Station. Sam had always had a disconcerting habit of getting his own way with very little apparent effort. On reflection, she wondered why she'd even bothered to argue.

However, telling herself she was giving in gracefully only as a means to an end didn't stop her from continuing to fume all the way as the train carried her to the small town of Brankstone. Nor did it prevent her promising herself that Sam would pay for this inconvenience — and pay dearly. Despite her determination to work during the journey, her laptop lay open and ignored in front of her as she seethed all over again at his high-handed manner.

Just who exactly did Sam Lawrence think he was? His CDs might finally be creeping up the country and western download charts, but recognition of his talent as a singer *was* only fairly recent, and still quite low-key. She was pleased for him, of course she was, because she was aware how hard he had worked for this taste of fame; but Roz had known him for too long, and knew him far too well, to be hugely impressed with his slowly growing celebrity status.

Sam still had a very long way to go

before he was anywhere near the same league as Brad Paisley or Nathan Carter, after all, and so Roz intended to remind him. His trouble was that he was evidently beginning to believe his own publicity, and thought he only had to say, 'Jump', and everyone around him would say, 'How high?' Well, she wasn't everyone, as he was about to discover.

What the guy badly needed was taking down a peg or two — and Roz had already decided she was just the one to do it. By the time she'd finished with him, he'd certainly think twice before issuing orders to her in that high-handed manner, Roz promised herself.

For all of her bad humour, Roz still couldn't deny the lifting of her spirits as the lush green of first the Hampshire, and then the Dorset, countryside came into view. Following swiftly was an eagerness to see her old home — and, of course, her great-aunt Ellen — again.

About Sam, she couldn't have cared

less, Roz assured herself stoutly. But see him she must, she supposed, if seeing him and talking to him would free her from an engagement that was little more than a joke these days — one that had gone on for far too long, and was no longer remotely funny.

It was a relief when the train pulled into the familiar station and Roz knew she was that much closer to setting her life in order. Treating this trip as a holiday had been the right — the only — thing to do, because even she had to admit a visit was long overdue. Once she had convinced Sam to see reason over the engagement business, she could enjoy the remainder of the time spent in her great-aunt's company, before returning to London and her life there with a clear conscience.

Roz could already picture herself boarding a train back to London from the opposite platform in a much happier frame of mind. She was smiling at the thought as she closed her laptop, collected her bags, and went to exit the train. She reached out to open the door-release catch in a much better humour than the one she had started the journey in.

Her feet had barely touched the station platform before she found herself swept up into a bear hug that lifted her and her belongings at least six inches above the ground, and quite squeezed the breath out of her lungs. She allowed herself to savour the moment briefly, resolutely refusing to analyse the rush of feeling evoked by those strong, possessive and all-too-familiar arms.

'Put me down, you big oaf.' She found herself laughing in spite of her determination to be severe with him from the outset. 'Stop it, Sam. People are looking.'

They were, too. A couple were actually going so far as to stare and point — but not at Roz, of that she was quite certain. If this was a taste of reflected glory, she wasn't at all keen, and she knew she'd never get used to the idea that people might actually recognise Sam in the street. She just hoped they stopped at looking and didn't start snapping on their mobile phones. Roz felt only relief when one of them shook her head — obviously doubting that even a minor celebrity could possibly be standing in a small town station — and pushed her friend onto the train Roz had just alighted from.

'Let them look.' Sam easily dismissed any real or imagined interest, setting her down and holding her at arm's length. The gaze resting on her face was steady and warm, and having him look at her in just such a way made her pulse behave in a most peculiar manner. It raced and jolted until she felt quite dizzy, and then he said softly, 'Hello, darlin'.'

'Hi.' To Roz's annoyance, she sounded all breathy and girlish, most unlike her usual brisk and efficient self.

Sam had taken her unawares, she told herself. She wasn't expecting him to meet her, and it was the element of surprise that had thrown her. That and, if she were honest with herself, the fact that he looked so — so . . . She hunted for a description that suited him; and, finding not a single one that did him justice, just stared back at him instead.

As ever, he towered above her own — not exactly meagre — five feet seven inches. She had to tilt her head back to look into a face that really was impossibly good-looking — a detail she had decided on without reservation a very long time ago.

Sam's features were lean; chiselled, almost, from skin, bone and sinew. His nose, well-shaped and very straight, jutted proudly above a full and sensual mouth. The thick, dark hair had been raked back carelessly, as always, by a hasty hand. Roz sometimes felt the action was a nervous gesture — if she could bring herself to believe that Sam possessed any nerves — but still often wondered if he owned a comb. Dark brows winged above eyes of a most unusual tawny shade, lit by tiny amber specks that seemed to brighten or dim to suit a given mood.

So, there he stood, tall, slim and straight. Dressed in denim jeans that clung to his thighs lovingly and a thin sweater that was moulded to the unexpected width of his chest and shoulders, it was little wonder, after all, that every female eye on the station was turned his way. Even the middle-aged lady serving coffee in the kiosk was gawping.

Roz gulped and reminded herself forcefully that *she* was not here to savour Sam's appearance, impressive though it might appear to some. She was here to end, once and for all, an engagement that should never have been allowed to happen in the first place.

'You're looking great,' he said, smiling down at her with admiration and approval showing clearly in his eyes.

Roz took a firm step back, refusing to

allow her toes to curl in her shoes as they were showing an annoying tendency of doing. In a carefully flippant tone, she accepted the compliment. 'Really? Well, I suppose you don't look so bad yourself. Shall we get on?'

Sam took the hint and, relieving her of her bags, suggested, 'Coffee, a drink, or straight back to the B&B?'

'I'd like to go straight home,' she said, smiling in spite of herself, and savouring the warmth the word always engendered in the secret, and often ignored, recesses of her heart.

Was it possible, she wondered idly as they made their way to the car park, to belong so completely to two places so entirely different that they might have been in different countries?

When she was in London, as Roz would freely admit, she had no desire to be anywhere else. She loved her life there: the bustling streets, the theatres, restaurants and shops; her smart apartment; her rising position in the human resources department of a large company; all of her City friends; and, of course, Andrew.

Yet the minute she returned to Dorset, with its gentler pace and beautiful surroundings, she always felt it was where she truly belonged, and wondered how she could bear to live anywhere else or stay away for as long as she did.

Perhaps she was two people, she mused, or perhaps she just had the happy knack of being at home anywhere. She hoped it was the latter, because if her life went according to her own meticulous planning, it was definitely in the City that her future lay.

'I like your hair like that.' Sam's approving murmur forced Roz to focus her attention on him once more.

Ruffling the short, artfully-tousled layers self-consciously, she managed a light laugh, taunting, 'Liar. You always liked my hair long.'

'It suits you,' was all he said, throwing her bags carelessly into the back of a familiar and very battered

Volvo estate car, and then opening the passenger door with a grand flourish to the shriek of protesting hinges.

For all the world, Roz thought wryly, as if it were a limousine. She couldn't prevent herself from mocking, 'Still using Aunt Ellen's transport, I see. Haven't you ever thought about bringing your own car with you, or even getting the WD-40 out on this one once in a while?'

He grinned, with no hint of embarrassment. 'She likes me to make use of her pride and joy when I'm here. In fact,' he added, lowering his tone confidingly, 'Ellen likes having me around.'

*And isn't that just the truth?* Roz admitted, recognising that *that* fact must be part of the problem Sam was insisting they had. Her great-aunt's deep and very obvious affection for Sam certainly wasn't going to make it easy for Roz to dismiss him summarily from her life.

Aloud, she said caustically, 'Only

because you butter her up all the time and let her spoil you.'

'Perhaps,' he agreed; and suddenly serious, added with a straight look in her direction, 'She doesn't get much chance to spoil you these days, Roz, does she?'

It was the first hint of any criticism that Sam had allowed to creep into his tone. Roz found it troubled her all the more because she had to admit that it was all too well-deserved.

'I don't have a career like yours,' she reminded him defensively, her eyes narrowing. 'I can't just take off at the end of every tour and rush home as and when the feeling moves me. I have commitments and set holiday entitlements.'

The statement was quite unfair, and Roz knew it. London was a scant two hours away by rail, and there were always weekends. She pulled the door closed hastily, cutting off any comment to that effect he might have cared to make. Fastening the seatbelt, she stared carefully ahead as Sam climbed into the driver's seat. Thankfully, he kept any such observations to himself.

The car, for all its great age, started — as always — first time. They were both silent as Sam negotiated filter lanes leading onto a roundabout, and then joined the heavy afternoon traffic heading out of Brankstone town centre. When they were well on their way, and he had still refrained from voicing any further opinion regarding her very infrequent visits home, Roz knew that she had to speak herself, or burst.

'All right,' she said acidly, as if he had just spoken first. 'You're right. I know it — and you know it. I *should* come home more often.'

Sam remained silent, but a dark eyebrow lifted expressively, and his mouth rearranged itself into a wry line. Though careful not to look directly at him, Roz saw every movement from the corner of her eye. She cringed inwardly, suddenly very aware of her own selfishness as seen from his persepctive.

'How is Aunt Ellen? She always sounds so well and cheerful on the phone that I suppose I don't worry enough about her. I know that I should, especially given her age,' she added quietly.

He seemed to relent then, and with a warm smile, said, 'Oh, you know Ellen, she'll outlive us all. She's thrilled to bits that you're coming, though of course she doesn't know why.'

With a jolt, Roz was suddenly reminded again of the reason for her visit, and that it wasn't only a social one. Just as well, she told herself, that she'd managed to arrange to take her annual leave this early in the year. It would give her time, once she had sorted things out with Sam, to bring her great-aunt round to her way of thinking, and also to keep her company for a while.

Not that Aunt Ellen lacked company of course, with the popular bed-and-breakfast establishment she owned and ran keeping her busy pretty well all the year round. Still, Roz supposed it wasn't the same as having family around, and even Sam wasn't that, strictly speaking.

Turning in the seat, and looking at the perfectly sculpted profile, she said firmly, 'We have to talk, Sam. 'Come to Dorset', you said. Well, now I'm here, at your insistence, and I won't be put off any longer. Just tell me what you think the problem is, so we can deal with it, end this ridiculous masquerade, and get on with our lives.'

'We've arrived,' Sam pointed out, as the old car swerved into a wide sweeping driveway and pulled up with a slight skid and scattering of gravel, 'and here's Ellen, so any discussion will just have to wait a little longer, I'm afraid.'

Roz couldn't argue with that, nor would she have wanted to prevent the wide smile she could feel lifting her lips. Great-aunt Ellen was poised on the porch step, leaning forward eagerly, and waving for all she was worth. The very minute Roz was out of the car she was clasped to a bony, crimplene-covered bosom, before being ushered into the large house that had been home for most of her childhood. Sam was left to carry the bags, she noted gleefully.

'Come on through, dear. It's still a bit chilly for the time of year, in spite of the sun. Now, sit yourself down and I'll make us a nice fresh pot of tea. Come on, Sam, you too.'

'I'll put these bags upstairs first,' he offered with surprisingly good grace. He didn't have to ask where to put them, since Roz's room was kept ready, and always had been. Unlike Sam's, it was never let out to paying guests.

With a contented sigh, Roz sat at the huge kitchen table that had always dominated the kitchen, and looked around. She felt the welcome heat from the old Aga warming her back, and watched her great-aunt bustling. With all the energy of a person half her age, she was hither and thither, putting the kettle on, setting a tray with the cups and saucers, and arranging home-made

17

scones on a plate without a pause.

It was a familiar and cosy domestic scene, and one that Roz wanted to enjoy after so long away. She tried hard to ignore the tiny fear niggling away at her subconscious, but finally she was forced to face and recognise it.

She had tried, at first, to tell herself that it was her imagination, that her great-aunt wasn't any older or any frailer than when she had last seen her several months before. Suddenly the regular phone calls home didn't seem nearly enough. Not when compared to the willing sacrifice made by a woman already of advancing years in offering an orphaned child a home.

Finally, facing for the first time the older woman's mortality, Roz felt an icy hand squeeze at her heart. With great reluctance, she was forced to accept that the woman who had brought her up with such loving care wasn't, after all, the invincible person she had always believed her to be.

She wanted to jump to her feet and

tell her beloved aunt to leave everything, that she would make the tea
while the older woman sat down and
allowed herself to be waited on.
Common sense kept her seated, and
told her in no uncertain terms that her
aunt would be mortally offended at any
suggestion that she couldn't manage
perfectly well, just as she always had.

Sam came in and sat down, and Roz
looked away from her aunt and raised
her stricken gaze to his face. She knew
her fear was showing but was quite
unable to find the strength to hide it.
Looking for comfort, for reassurance,
she found it in the warm clasp of
strong, tanned fingers, and a look that
was warning and yet understanding all
at once.

'There you are, a proper Dorset
cream tea. I know it's your favourite,
Rosalind, and the scones are still warm
from the Aga, just as you like them.'
The gentle tone with its slight hint of
the local dialect was soothingly normal,
and Roz tried hard to ignore the shade

of a tremor in the hands that set the tray on the table. She almost succeeded.

'That looks wonderful, Aunt Ellen.' Roz didn't have to invent the enthusiasm that showed in her voice. 'I can see you haven't lost your touch.'

'Of course not. I'm not in my dotage yet. I can still knock up a batch of scones with the best of them.'

'Better than most — you can still beat that neighbour of yours hands down,' Sam informed her with a twinkle, knowing, just as Roz did, of the rivalry that had always existed between the two guest houses.

'Well, she tries, you know, but she's getting on now, poor soul,' said Aunt Ellen sympathetically, completely ignoring the fact that she could easily give the woman several years.

The ensuing laughter lightened the atmosphere and Roz's heart, as she told herself stoutly that Aunt Ellen would go on forever. Of course she would. How old was she, after all? Roz was ashamed to say she really had no idea, because the subject was never discussed. If she stabbed a guess, she would have to place her aunt well into her eighties — but surely that made her a mere youngster in a day and age when everyone was fitter and living longer. She really was worrying for nothing. While she was here, though, Roz vowed, she would insist on helping out, overruling all of her aunt's usual objections to do so.

Aunt Ellen had always been far too independent. You only had to look at the way she'd made a single-handed success of the B&B. She was a businesswoman long before such a thing was generally accepted, making a name for herself and her 'bed-and-breakfast-with-optional-evening-meal' establishment in the seaside town of Brankstone through sheer hard work and determination.

It was hardly surprising, in Roz's admittedly biased opinion, that the same people returned year after year to sample Ellen's old-fashioned hospitality and home-cooked meals. Without exception, the guests happily forgave the fact that *Sea View* lacked even a glimpse of any such thing — and, indeed, was actually a long walk or a short car ride away from the nearest beach.

Roz was pretty sure that the meagre staff Ellen allowed herself during the busiest times would probably be happy to work for nothing — or at least very little. Her great-aunt was a tough but fair employer, expecting them to work every bit as hard as she did herself, but never demanding of them anything that she wouldn't do herself, either.

When it came to her great-niece, however, Aunt Ellen showed herself up for the traditionalist she really was. She tried to hide it, but it was quite obvious she was disappointed that Roz had grown up with the same independent streak she herself demonstrated. It would obviously have suited Ellen so much better if her beloved great-niece had settled into an early marriage with someone local, and concentrated on the raising of a brood of children.

It was partly the awareness of her great-aunt's wishes that had prompted Roz into the farcical engagement with Sam, and now — she sighed gustily at the thought — she was going to have to remind him, yet again, of the promise he had made at the time — and hold him to it.

Somehow, the rest of the day was gone, with a speed that left Roz wondering what had happened to it. She should have remembered, she mused ruefully, that there was rarely a quiet moment in the house, with guests continually in and out, and most of them eager to chat. There hadn't really been a convenient time to insist on discussing a matter that was becoming increasingly urgent — at least, as far as Roz was concerned — with Sam.

Finally alone in the room that had always been hers — her sanctuary in a busy household — Roz pressed the heat of her forehead against the cool glass of the window pane. She stared out across the darkening garden with a troubled expression on her face and a troubled feeling in her heart.

She was making excuses, and she knew it. There was nothing at all stopping her from marching down the landing, right that very moment, knocking on Sam's door, and refusing to leave until the whole thing was sorted out to their mutual satisfaction.

It sounded so easy, and it really should have been. They would merely be ending an arrangement that had suited them both for a time; but the very fact that Sam had brought her all the way home for a face-to-face confrontation convinced Roz that it was going to be anything but.

She sighed deeply. As a child, she had always put off doing anything distasteful until the very last minute; and now here she was at twenty-six years old, doing the self-same thing.

# 2

Roz leaned back and stared at the image reflected back at her in the bedroom window pane, mirror-like against the black of the night outside. Her eyes grew dreamy as the years rolled backwards.

She saw again the child who had first been given this room all of twenty years ago. She saw the bright hair, neatly braided; the snub nose that always seemed to be running; and the tears on the freckled face.

The sole survivor of the mangled wreckage of a minibus caught up in a motorway pile-up, in one fell swoop Roz had lost not only her parents, but both sets of grandparents too. She had turned, then, to the woman who was the only claim to family that she was left to her. Beneath the cloak of her great-aunt Ellen's kindness and patience, all those years ago, Roz had rediscovered the kind of caring, nurturing love she had thought lost to her forever.

'I can never take the place of any of them,' Aunt Ellen had explained gently, 'and I would never try.' She had taken the young Roz in her arms. 'But I hope we can be of comfort to each other. I love you dearly, Rosalind, and I'm very happy to have you to live with me.'

As young as she was, it hadn't taken Roz long to appreciate that her great-aunt had lost her own family too in that crash. It wasn't only a case of Roz needing someone, but of them needing each other. After that, she had settled into her great-aunt's large house and way of life with surprising ease.

Gradually, over the years, she had learned more about Ellen's past, and the explanation for how a woman on her own had come to be living in a house that was far too large for one person. The reason had nothing to do with commercial enterprise or ambition either, as Roz gradually discovered.

Harry and Ellen — Roz's maternal grandmother's only sister — had only been married and taken out a mortgage a short time before the Second World War broke out. They had chosen their future home intentionally for its size and seaside location. Both coming from small families, they were keen to have a large brood themselves, and considered that the Brankstone area had a lot to offer a growing family.

The couple had refused to contemplate the fact they might never have a future together, and the letters they sent were full of their hopes and dreams — but, like so many others, Ellen's young soldier husband had never returned.

She was already living in the house alone, and refused absolutely to sell it and buy somewhere smaller. She had never married again, but instead had filled the rooms with paying guests, and made the house she cherished into a career that had brought her many friends and a good income over the years.

It was watching the way her great-aunt had managed her life so successfully, with no help from the opposite sex, that had made Roz determined to do the same with her own. That there was more to life than marrying young and starting a family, she had no doubt at all. Like her aunt, Roz had a knack when dealing with people, quickly setting them at ease in her company.

After trying various other avenues, she eventually decided to put that knack to proper use in the field of human resources. Since making that decision, she had been gaining qualifications and steadily climbing the ladder toward her own personal goal of managing an HR department, possibly within a multinational company.

Roz became aware while she was still in her teens that, despite quite early successes in her chosen career, this was not what her aunt desired for her, despite the example she'd set and the support she willingly gave.

'It wasn't my choice to spend my life running a business alone,' Aunt Ellen had pointed out. 'If Harry had lived, my life as a wife and mother would have been very different. As it was, fate decreed that you became my family, and it was always wonderful for me to have you here. Times are different now, and you can have it all, my darling: a career, a man to love, and a family.'

It was hard for the teenage Roz to explain to the aunt that she adored that the future Ellen had mapped out for her didn't appeal at all. What she wanted was to be in charge of her own destiny — her own, and no-one else's. Maybe she would settle down eventually, but there was certainly no hurry. Meanwhile, she had a busy life and a happy one that she wasn't inclined to change any time soon.

It was hard to explain, and so she never did, but allowed Sam to convince her that a fake engagement was the answer for them both. As he pointed out, it would stop constant and annoying speculation about him regarding nonexistent romances, and allow him to concentrate on his music; while also keeping Aunt Ellen from fretting that Roz was missing out on a future family life.

What neither of them had considered was just how cruel it was to let the older woman go on hoping for the great-great-nephews and -nieces they would never give her, let her go on waiting for Roz to settle down the man of her dreams, when Roz and Sam knew that he wasn't that man. In fact, Roz was firmly convinced such a man did not exist.

An involuntary heartfelt sigh that came from deep within her brought Roz back to the present and to the young woman she was today — a woman whose reflection stared back at her with wide green eyes and a solemn expression.

Gone now were the freckles, as long as she stayed out of the sun. Her complexion these days was kept creamy and clear with the help of expensive cosmetics. Her nose no longer turned up, but was still small and straight. All in all, a pretty face, always expertly made up to suit her professional image, and usually smiling. The braids had long since been banished in favour of a series of modern hairstyles, the latest of which was the very short and carefully-tousled mop that suited both the thick, bright red waves and the slim features beneath it.

Roz considered with approval that she — in her smartly-cut navy suit — looked exactly what she was, a City girl through and through. It was only right that she should marry someone who belonged in the City too. Someone who understood her hectic way of life; someone who understood the fact that there was no such thing as set hours in her job; and, above all, understood the fact that she had no intention of trying

31

to juggle babies and other family commitments with a demanding career. Not for a very long time, if ever.

Andrew had all of those qualities. He was the ideal partner for Roz, and had taken some finding. Theirs would be a marriage of two like minds, between two totally fulfilled and very ambitious people. Yet somehow, although that sounded wonderful to Roz, she was convinced that Aunt Ellen would not be impressed.

She shook her head dolefully and sighed. Her window pane image did the same. No, Aunt Ellen would not be impressed at all, because she already had her heart set on a happy-ever-after for Roz — as Sam's wife.

* ★ ★

After a good night's sleep, however, Roz managed to convince herself that if she could only bring Sam around to her point of view, it would only be a matter of time before, between them, they could get Aunt Ellen to do the same. She had always set great store by everything Sam said and did, though heaven only knew why. He wasn't family, after all; just someone who came to stay once upon a time, and never really went away.

Roz found herself dressing, rather self-consciously, in a way that she knew he would like. Discarding another smart suit and silk blouse in favour of close-fitting denim jeans and a baggy, bright yellow sweatshirt she found in the back of the wardrobe, she went downstairs.

'Why, you look like Spring itself,' Aunt Ellen approved, before coaxing, 'Take these breakfasts in to the guests for me, will you, love? It'll start their day a treat to be waited on by a bright young thing, instead of someone as long in the tooth as me.'

Roz dropped a kiss onto the crown of frizzy white hair that her aunt never quite managed to tame, and lifting the loaded tray she turned towards the door and came face to face with Sam coming in.

Obviously fresh from the shower, judging by the way the sleek dark hair curled damply around his ears, he looked, as always, just too disturbingly handsome for his own good. Since he had a voice to match his looks, it was hardly surprising that he was so much in demand with the ladies who made up the bulk of his audiences, or that his career had recently taken off with surprising speed.

In the tiny pause before she walked past him, Roz didn't miss the appreciation in the gaze that swiftly took in her appearance, nor could she halt the tide of hot colour that swept up over her jawbone and right up into her tousled hair in response to that look.

Why on earth he should be able to affect her like that, she really had no idea. He was just a man; and, for all his good looks, not *her* kind of man at all, and never had been. Sam was, and always had been, absolutely fine as a friend, but nothing more. Oh, no, nothing more.

Roz was far too busy serving breakfasts to stop and ask herself just why she was so vehement about that. By the time she returned to the kitchen, she had forgotten all about it — but not about her intention to get Sam securely on her side as soon as possible.

'Good morning, Sam,' she wished him belatedly, positively beaming at him. 'What can I get for you? Coffee, black and strong, just as you like it?'

The tawny eyes peered at her suspiciously over the paper he was perusing. If he was surprised at this sudden change in her attitude, he managed to hide it very successfully, only saying mildly, 'That would be very acceptable, thank you, but I can easily get it myself.'

'I don't mind this once.' Roz smiled, adding under her breath: 'But I don't intend to make a habit of it, believe me.'

She poured coffee and made freshly-scrambled eggs on the slightly burnt toast that he always favoured. With growing impatience, she allowed him to devour it at his leisure with every appearance of enjoyment, before enquiring, very politely, after his plans for the day.

'Why do you want to know, Roz?' He couldn't keep the curiosity from his voice. 'What did you have in mind? You *do* have something in mind, I take it?'

She shrugged carelessly. 'I just thought we might do something together.'

He glanced at her beautifully-manicured, bronze-painted fingernails, before saying in a wry tone, making no attempt to hide his amusement, 'I was going to weed the garden and do a bit of pruning, but you're very welcome to join me.'

He was laughing at her. Laughing right up the sleeve of that damn checked shirt, she realised furiously. He knew they had to talk. It had been his own idea that they get together for that very purpose, and now he was intentionally making it as difficult for her as ever he could.

Roz swallowed her chagrin and fury with the greatest of difficulty, realising, even as her temper steadily rose, that it wouldn't do to get on the wrong side of him. He could make things even more awkward for her than they already were, and she was well aware of it. She still determined, there and then, that he wouldn't get the better of her, no matter how hard he tried.

'I'd like that.' She smiled sweetly, and hid a grin when he couldn't keep the look of surprise from his face.

'Gardening?' Aunt Ellen had obviously been earwigging, and now she bustled to the table, setting her old brown teapot down with a bang. 'Gardening?' she repeated indignantly. 'On your first holiday here for months? Oh, no, I won't hear of it. I shall get round to it, just as I always have.'

'And just why should you get all the fun, Ellen,' Sam interrupted, 'when you know how I love to garden?'

You couldn't help but admire him, Roz allowed reluctantly, as Aunt Ellen gave in gracefully, totally convinced by his easy and persuasive manner that she really was actually doing him a favour.

'But you won't get Rosalind out there.' Ellen shook her head emphatically. 'She's having you on, my lad, she's always hated gardening.'

'I need the fresh air,' Roz insisted quickly, 'and I shall be out there just as soon as I've helped you clear up in here.' She wanted to ask if there were gardening gloves she could borrow, but couldn't quite face the derision from Sam that such a request would bring.

'I'll get the tools ready and make a start, then.' Sam swallowed the last mouthful of his coffee as he rose from the table in one fluid movement. Roz couldn't help watching him as he stretched like a supple cat before strolling leisurely from the room. It was only with great difficulty that she

38

turned her attention to the loading of a brand-new dishwasher that sat gleaming whitely, totally at odds with the rest of the old-fashioned kitchen.

Her aunt had always been dead against such modern appliances, but its arrival was explained away — when Roz asked — as a present from Sam that she didn't have the heart to refuse, followed by a confession that it was proving very useful. Slightly miffed, Roz wished she had thought of it; but, on reflection, she doubted she'd have managed to get her aunt to accept it so easily.

With Sam out of the way, Roz enjoyed a comfortable chat with her great-aunt as they worked efficiently, side by side. She was just wishing that she could have been more of a companion to the woman who had given her so much, more the sort of person her great-aunt might have wished her to be, when her thoughts were scattered asunder as the older woman spoke.

'I can guess why you're home,' Ellen

suddenly said knowingly, the lined face creasing into a pleased smile, 'and it's about time this was sorted out, too, if you ask me.'

She knew! Roz stared at Ellen in amazement. She had always known that her great-aunt was shrewd, but that she should have guessed . . . Well, either that, or Sam had done the decent thing and broken it to her gently himself.

Relief flooded through Roz until she felt quite weak, and exceptionally light-headed at the thought that Ellen might even have guessed there was another man in Roz's life. It was going to be all right. There was no need for the lengthy explanations she had prepared, over and over, in her head, because Aunt Ellen somehow knew. It was obvious from her manner that she understood the engagement had run its course and it was time for them to call it a day.

'Yes.' The older woman's smile widened, until her whole face was filled with bright pleasure. 'You've come home to set the date. I really couldn't be happier. You're finally going to marry Sam — and not a day too soon.'

41

# 3

Roz couldn't believe it. Aunt Ellen had somehow convinced herself that her great-niece had come home for the sole purpose of making the arrangements for her wedding to Sam.

She had no idea what she replied to her aunt's preposterous, yet quite understandable, assumption; no idea at all. Too late, she realised she should have seen this coming a mile away — in her aunt's eyes, it would be extremely strange for a six-year engagement to end any other way but in marriage.

Somehow, Roz managed to murmur something noncommittal before she excused herself and dashed from the room, nearly knocking one of the guests flying in her haste.

'This is Sam's fault,' she fumed aloud, when she had reached the comparative safety of her room, and recovered her powers of speech.

She found herself pacing from window to wall, from wall to door, and back again, wishing fervently that she hadn't long ago given up the childhood habit of biting her nails. Roz didn't smoke — never had — but accepted quite readily that this situation could almost have justified her taking the habit up.

Reaching the window again and looking out, she was treated to the sight of Sam's broad back bent over the flower bed below her room. Refusing to allow herself to get side-tracked by the tantalising glimpse of tanned flesh where his shirt had pulled out of his waistband, she glared at him so fiercely she almost expected to see two burn holes appear in his clothes.

'*Your* fault,' she confirmed, and spinning on her heel, went straight down to tackle him, while her anger and dismay were still at fever pitch.

'Aunt Ellen only thinks we're on the verge of setting the date for our wedding,' she said without preamble, stopping close behind him, with her legs apart and her hands firm on her slim hips.

He didn't even turn round, she noticed wrathfully, just carried right on weeding as he said, in the most reasonable tone, 'That's hardly surprising, since we *are* engaged and have been for some time.'

'We are *not*,' she denied hotly, and then hurried on: 'Well — we are — but we aren't really — as *you* very well know.'

It all sounded very feeble even to her own ears, and Roz was becoming crosser and hotter by the minute. She shouldn't have to explain to him, he knew better than anyone exactly what she meant and exactly how things stood.

She stamped her foot, which was a little pointless as it made no sound at all on the grass, and hissed, 'Oh, *will* you stop doing what you're doing and turn round when I'm talking to you?'

Sam stood up. He then straightened his back with all the speed of a man at least fifty years older, inch by maddening inch, before — finally — he turned to face her.

'You sound annoyed,' he said, and she was pleased to see that at least he wasn't smiling.

If he had been . . . well, her fingers were just itching to make contact with that smooth, tanned cheek. With difficulty, she clenched her hands into tight fists, and held on to her temper.

'This was all *your* idea,' she told him, looking him straight in the eye. '*You* got us into this mess with your stupid idea, and you can damn well get us out of it. This engagement was *never* meant to end in marriage, as you very well know, and now Aunt Ellen is looking for us to start making arrangements. What are we going to *do*, Sam?'

The speech that had started so well, in a calmly reasonable tone, ended on a wobbly note that was almost a wail of sheer terror. Sam took a step forward, his hands already reaching out to comfort her.

'Don't touch me.' Her own hands were thrust out, palms facing him in clear repudiation.

'All right.' His arms went up in surrender. 'So, let's talk. We'll start with you telling me what *you* think we should do, shall we? And go on from there.'

Roz took a deep breath. This was better, at last she was getting somewhere, and he was being sensible for once. All she had to do was to state the case, exactly as it was, and then they could deal with the situation in which they found themselves in a reasonable and adult manner.

'This engagement,' she began, 'which, incidentally, and as I continually have to remind you, *was* all your idea. You do remember that, don't you? It was meant to be simply a matter of convenience. It was arranged, on the one hand, to stop Aunt Ellen fretting over the lack of anyone resembling husband material hovering on my horizon; and on the other hand, it would supposedly stop overzealous reporters inventing love interests for you. Or that's what you told me at the time.'

'Right,' Sam agreed readily enough.

'Right,' Roz repeated, 'and we made a bargain at the time that, should either of us meet someone that we really wanted to marry, the engagement would simply be called off.'

'We did.'

Roz sighed; he might sound ever so reasonable, but he wasn't exactly helping. It looked as if she was going to have to spell it out for him, word by word.

'I've now met someone that I do wish to marry; as I've already told you, Sam. Therefore, our engagement, or arrangement — call it what you will — must be terminated.'

'But it's not that simple any more, is it?'

He looked serious enough now, she thought; that was for sure. In fact, the expression on his face frightened her.

What did he mean? What was he saying? Surely he didn't expect her to actually marry him? That would be carrying something that had started as little more than a joke a bit too far.

'Of course it's that simple,' she told him tartly. 'All we have to do is to tell anyone who's interested that the engagement is off because I've met someone else. It happens all the time, Sam, it's no big deal.'

'It wasn't then — it is now. Roz, I think you're forgetting just how long this has been going on, and how much has changed.' For a moment he looked as confused as she felt, and he reached up a hand to rake it distractedly through his dark hair. 'It's been six years,' he reminded her gently. 'Six years of everyone thinking of us as a couple . . . '

'So,' she interrupted with a careless shrug, 'it's been six years — so what?'

'I'm not the same person I was then, not as anonymous, and Ellen is six years older . . . '

48

'You want to continue with a phoney engagement because you're a bit of a name on the country and western circuit now, and because Aunt Ellen is in her eighties.' She glared at him in disbelief and, huffing loudly, went on: 'I don't believe I'm hearing this.' She shook her head. 'I really don't.

'The press and social media will crucify you, and speculation will be rife if we put it out that you broke it off. You know what the tabloids are like. They'll have a field day, be all over this place like a measles rash, delving into our lives and background. They've only left us alone thus far because we lead such apparently boring lives. Something like this might cause the sort of scandal that could kill Ellen at her age — and I shouldn't have to remind you that, in fact, she is actually in her *nineties* — if you breaking off the engagement didn't do that first.'

He was deadly serious, and the words held a ring of truth that couldn't be denied. Shock made Roz's mouth drop open, and rooted her feet to the damp grass. All around, the birds went on singing, a watery sun went on shining, and flowers went on blooming just as they always did on any normal spring day in Brankstone.

Except this, Roz didn't have to remind herself, was not any normal day in Brankstone, or anywhere else. In fact, she was beginning to feel as if nothing in her life would ever be normal again. They'd carelessly let the stupid, childish arrangement go on for far too long, and now it seemed that it was far too late to try and get out of it easily.

It was all to have been so simple, as easy, as the breaking of a contract that had never even been official, or ever signed; and now, with a few well-chosen words, Sam had shown her that it wasn't going to be simple at all. If he was to be believed, it was going to be nigh on impossible — or was it?

Roz decided that she was made of sterner stuff than to give up just like that. He must be made to spell out, word by word, exactly what he intended that they should do, because even he must realise that something *had* to be done. She would listen, give him a fair hearing, and then she would make up her own mind. He didn't own her — he never had — and, she told herself firmly, he never would.

'So — ' She was calm now, and quite in control of the emotions that his bald statement had momentarily scattered to the four winds. ' — what exactly are you saying, Sam?'

'I'm *suggesting*,' he emphasised the word, 'that for the time being we will just have to stay engaged.'

She'd known it, she was even expecting it — and yet hearing it spoken like that was a much bigger shock than she had ever dreamed it would be. The very thought of doing as he suggested was more than she could take. Things had changed — she had changed — she wanted *out* and she wanted out *now*.

'*What?*' Her voice was so shrill that she even glanced over her shoulder, fearful lest Aunt Ellen should hear her from the house; then, lowering her tone, she hissed, 'Stay engaged indefinitely? Are you quite mad? I will not do it. I want out of this engagement, Sam, right now, and you had just better find a way.'

Her piece said, Roz bent to snatch a trowel from the flower bed, before storming across the garden to begin weeding furiously at a point as far away from him as she could get.

# 4

'My word, you have got a lot done.'

It was Aunt Ellen's soft voice that finally penetrated the chaotic jumble of thoughts and impressions that had been chasing round, in ever more muddled directions, inside a head that had begun to throb painfully. The note of pleasure and admiration made Roz look along a surprising length of border that had been tackled with the trowel and was totally weed-free. The bucket nearby was overflowing.

'So I have,' she agreed with a wry grin; and, pleased in spite of herself, she sat back on her heels and accepted the mug that her aunt held out to her.

'But you've ruined your lovely hands, dear.' The older woman shook her head in dismay. 'And spoiled your pretty nails.'

'Oh, they'll scrub up.' Roz dismissed

the scratched and filthy fingers and chipped nail varnish easily, fully accepting that they were going to be the least of her worries. Her real problem was not going to be solved with soap and water and another coat of nail polish, and the hours of toiling in the garden had done nothing towards finding a solution.

Her aunt seemed to hesitate before she spoke again, and then the words were said in a rush. 'I thought I heard you and Sam quarrelling earlier. I do hope you haven't had a serious falling-out.' It was said lightly, but Roz didn't miss the anxiety in the faded blue of the older woman's eyes, or the worried question in her tone.

She longed to say that, yes, they had fallen out, that the engagement was off, and that she didn't care if she never saw Sam Lawrence again as long as she lived. She longed to say it, and let him do what he would about it. Her aunt, too, would get over it, she was sure, but she didn't deserve to have it thrown at her in such a fashion. She didn't deserve to be lied to in the way that they had all those years ago, either, and allowing it to continue for so long only made things a million times worse.

What had seemed funny back then, and harmless, was shown up clearly now for what it was: the deceiving of someone who didn't deserve to be deceived, someone who had always been painfully and totally honest — and someone who had tried to bring her up to be the same. Roz was suddenly bitterly ashamed, both of herself and Sam, and she wished with all of her heart that she could turn the clock back six years. She would welcome being given the chance, back then, to handle the situation with the total honesty it deserved.

Aunt Ellen was waiting quietly for her answer, a little concerned, but obviously completely unaware of the turmoil going on in Roz's head. A worried frown furrowed the older woman's brow, and Roz knew suddenly that Sam was right. It wasn't easy for her to face that, but face it she had to, and with better grace than she had shown so far. Behaving like a spoilt brat would solve nothing, she saw at last, and nor would putting all the blame on Sam's shoulders help.

From somewhere, she dredged up a warm smile, rubbed her aching back with a dirty hand, and said lightly, 'Oh, you know Sam, Aunt Ellen, bossy as always. I'm not having him telling me where to work in my own garden.'

She must have sounded convincing, because her aunt threw back her head and laughed with every appearance of enjoyment, before collecting the empty mug and walking away chuckling, pausing only to say over her shoulder, 'Lunch will be in an hour, dear.'

As soon as she had disappeared round the side of the house, Roz got slowly and a little stiffly to her feet. What she meant to do was not going to be easy, but she knew that it had to be done. Her display of temper earlier had been unnecessary, and unforgivable, and now she was going to have to pay for it — by eating humble pie in great unappetising chunks.

'I'm sorry.'

She didn't mean to sound ungracious, but her apology sounded abrupt even to her own ears. She almost flinched in readiness for the scathing comment she was sure was coming.

'That's all right.'

Sam looked up from the shrub he was pruning with a smile that took her breath away. It was a smile so warm and genuine that there was no doubting his forgiveness, or the fact that he had actually understood why she had behaved in such a way.

'No, it's not — not really,' she said ruefully, looking up at him and trying to ignore the traitorous racing of a pulse that could be so easily influenced by the charming smile that she should have grown used to long ago. 'No matter what the provocation, there's never any excuse for behaving like a shrew.'

'You were upset, and I know that's a pathetic understatement, but it's the best that I can do. You obviously hadn't given too much thought to the conse-quences of breaking off such an increasingly well-known, and long-standing, engagement.'

'No.'

'To be honest, neither had I. What we should have decided at the time was just how long it would be sensible to let this, erm, *arrangement* go on for. We were careless, but who can blame us? After all, engagements are broken off every day, without anyone paying much heed.

'We both knew it was only ever meant to be a temporary thing, just to give us time to get our lives organised. What we should have realised was, the longer ours went on for, the more difficult it would become to break things off without upsetting Ellen and also attracting unwanted attention from the media as my name became known.'

Roz was surprised, and she looked at him with new respect. He understood — he really did — and that made her feel a whole lot better about the situation they had found themselves in. At least, she acknowledged, he wasn't just being plain awkward, and she had, at first, really thought that he was. All they had to do was to give the matter some careful thought, and together they could surely find a solution.

'Tell me about him,' Sam went on quietly, 'this guy who has stolen your heart. He must be quite a man, I'm sure, since you were always so dead set on remaining single — until now.'

Roz was unaware of the way her attractive face lit up, or of the sudden stillness in Sam's tawny eyes as he watched her.

'Well, honestly, I never dreamed that I'd ever meet someone who was so exactly right for me.' Her voice was full of enthusiasm as she went on eagerly, 'His name is Andrew Reynolds and he

59

has fair hair, blue eyes, and is just a couple of years older than me. He's very good-looking,' she added.

'So,' Sam's mouth twisted into a wry grin, 'I know his name, and what he looks like, but what I don't know yet is what makes you so sure that he's the right man for you.'

Roz laughed good-naturedly, pleased that he was taking an interest. Suddenly sure he would soon agree that Andrew was just the person that she needed in her life.

'He works for the same company, but in a different department; though, of course, he's further up the promotion ladder than I am. He's as dedicated to improving his prospects as I am to bettering mine.'

Sam was silent, his face expressionless, and he just nodded slightly to show that he was listening as he waited for Roz to go on.

'That's the wonderful thing — ' She laughed. ' — he's so supportive and understanding of everything that I do, and he is just as keen for me to get on as I am. Andrew takes me to all the right parties, making sure that we meet all the right people. He understands about ambition, about career moves, and the need to be totally dedicated and on call in case any opportunity is missed. He wouldn't want a stay-at-home wife — any more than I'd want to be one — and he says that I'm a great asset to a career-minded man.'

She paused, breathless from delivering what was almost a speech, and looked expectantly up at Sam, waiting for the comment she was sure would be forthcoming. When it came, it was so unexpected that it almost shocked her.

'Sounds great — but what about love?' he asked briefly, his tone flat as, without moving so much as a muscle, he waited for her answer.

'We — well, of course I *love* him . . . ' She wasn't aware of the slight hesitation in her reply as she quickly warmed to her theme. ' . . . and he loves me, of course he does, because we're so very right for each other.'

'It doesn't sound much like *love* to me,' Sam emphasised. 'It sounds more like a business merger.'

Roz was taken aback, but only for a moment before anger raced to the rescue, and she said bitingly, 'Oh, and you'd know all about love, would you, Sam? I didn't realise that you were an expert.'

He didn't even have the grace to look embarrassed, she noticed, as he said, 'Well, I've had my moments; and believe me, balance sheets and career moves weren't a part of them. I thought love was mutual attraction — shared interests, maybe — but also finding the same things funny, and not just pushing each other up the career ladder for a swift and lucrative promotion.'

He made it all sound so clinical, impersonal even, and Roz found herself frowning before she denied hotly, 'It's not like that at all.'

'Isn't it? So what is it like then, Roz?' He was watching her curiously, waiting for her answer — an answer that she suddenly found that she didn't have, much to her own consternation.

'It's . . . ' Her mind searched furiously for something to say, something to take that self-righteous look right off his face, and could only come up with a feeble: ' . . . it's a meeting of like minds.'

'*Minds?*' he said scathingly, staring at her for a moment in disbelief before taking a step forward. Lowering his head to look deep into her eyes, he asked, so softly that she had to strain to hear, 'And what about hearts, Roz? What about hearts?'

He was standing close — far, far too close for Roz's peace of mind — so she could see the tiny bright flecks in eyes that saw too much, and knew her too well. She should come back at him with a snappy answer that would put him in his place, she knew. She should move away, put a safe space between them. She knew that, too, but her feet seemed to be rooted deeply into the damp earth, and she could only stand and stare.

'Does seeing him across a room make your pulse beat faster?' The question was little more than a whisper, and she watched, mesmerised, as a tanned hand reached out to caress her own. 'Does his touch bring you alive? When he kisses you, how do you feel? Do you feel like this?'

Roz knew what was coming. She felt, somehow, that she had always known it would come to this. Had known from the moment he had demanded that they discuss the ridiculous farce of an engagement face to face, instead of just calling it off and making an announcement to that effect, as she had wished. She knew, long before Sam bent his head to hers, that he was going to kiss her — and still she was powerless to stop him — even if she had wanted to.

She had been kissed before, of course, on lots of occasions, and by Sam on quite a few of them, but never like this. No, never, ever, like this, and very definitely not by Andrew.

His lips were gentle, but she knew that already. What she hadn't known — or expected — was the way his lips moulded to her own as if they belonged there, coaxing her own to part with the merest pressure, and yet with a passion that was undeniable.

Roz swayed into the arms that were waiting to gather her close, welcomed the hands that caressed her closer, until she was shockingly aware of the heat being generated by two bodies that had almost merged into one.

She was lost in wonder, boneless and pliant in his arms. Aware only of sensations that started at the soles of her tingling feet, making her toes curl involuntarily inside her shoes, and moving on until her whole body was alive as she was sure it had never been before.

Heat burned, suddenly and unexpectedly, along veins that had always remained consistently cool in the past when she was in any man's arms. For the very first time that she could remember, Roz felt a fierce yearning that far outweighed reason and left her wanting more — much, much more.

Sam lifted his head, and her sense of loss was so overwhelming that she heard herself moan softly. He smiled; and then gently, but firmly, placed her from him, and looked at her with the gravest expression on his handsome face.

'Is that,' he asked, 'how *he* makes you feel?'

Roz couldn't answer — she had no answer. She stared up at him with wide, startled eyes for a very long minute; and then, without a word, she turned and ran, knowing only that she had to get away.

And yet, even as she fled, she was forced to ask herself if she was running away from Sam — or from herself and the feelings he had aroused in her.

# 5

Wild-eyed, Roz stared at her flushed and dishevelled reflection in the bathroom mirror. She'd come tearing up the stairs, ostensibly to tidy herself up for lunch. A lunch that was, even now, probably prepared and laid out most attractively on the table in the big kitchen below, waiting to be eaten.

Roz didn't know how she was going to force herself back down there, never mind find an appetite to eat anything. Dirty hands remained unwashed, tangled hair uncombed, as she looked at herself, and went on looking through narrowed and wary eyes.

A stranger gazed back at her. A young woman with fire still burning through her veins — a young woman with full, rosy lips that had very evidently and very recently been thoroughly kissed, and were still tingling from the attention they had received. Attention that Roz could not deny had been very welcome, and — to her utter embarrassment — she had not even attempted to hide it.

She'd never be able to face Sam again. Indeed, her face grew hot and red at the very thought. How he must be laughing, she taunted herself, at the way she had fallen into his hands like the ripest plum falling from the tree. It wasn't only that she had let him kiss her — though that was bad enough, for heaven's sake — it was the fact that she had clearly not only enjoyed the whole experience, but kissed him back, and made everything a million times worse.

Roz scrubbed a dirty hand across those offending lips, as if she could wipe away the feel of Sam's mouth on hers. All she succeeded in doing was to leave smeary black marks behind like a comical moustache. In no mood to find it funny, she slapped the mirror in front of her, and then shrieked in quite ridiculous fury as the grimy prints transferred to the glass.

'He can't do this to me,' she fumed aloud, the words echoing hollowly around the small bathroom, 'and I won't let him. He's breaking all the rules, but he will not get the better of me no matter *how* he tries, or *what* he tries. I don't know what game he's playing, but whatever it is, he won't win it.'

They were determined words, full of self-righteous indignation, and she meant every one of them. However, Roz still did not feel able to confront the man who had caused all of her turmoil until she had showered, washed her hair, reapplied her make-up, and dressed herself in city clothes. The effort was worth it. It seemed to reaffirm her own personality, and give her back the previous confidence in her future that one kiss had all but destroyed.

'Oh, there you are.' Aunt Ellen looked up from the pastry she was rolling, and then said, with a hint of a smile in her voice, 'I thought you went to wash your hands, dear, not to get dressed up for lunch. You make me feel quite shabby.'

'Everything was so dirty, and I was so hot . . . ' Roz found herself quickly on the defensive, before her aunt interrupted her flood of ready-prepared excuses with a mild, 'I was only joking, dear. You look quite lovely. Go and sit down, and let me help you to lunch.'

'I'll do it,' Roz insisted. 'I only hope it's not ruined by my inconsiderate behaviour.' She looked round, almost fearfully, before asking, 'Where's Sam? Has he had his?'

'It's only soup and crusty bread — ' The rolling pin was set in motion once more. ' — hard to spoil that; and yes, Sam's had his and is back hard at work. I told him it would ruin his digestion, but you know Sam.'

Well, I thought I did, but now I'm beginning to wonder, Roz mused as she helped herself to home-made soup that was full of all kinds of vegetables and tender pieces of meat, and then to thick slices of bread that had been freshly baked that morning. And, she fumed silently, I hope his digestion *does* suffer, because he's probably made sure that mine will.

'Remember when Sam first came here?' Aunt Ellen had the light of nostalgia in her eyes as she expertly covered neatly-sliced apple with pastry, 'Must be all of seven years ago. He said then that my soup was the best he had ever tasted.'

They were both silent as they each viewed the picture she had conjured up of the tall, lean man who had turned up at the door looking for lodgings, complete with scruffy holdall and immaculate guitar.

He must have been about the same age as she was now, Roz realised, and she remembered that he had been dressed all in faded denim with a battered cowboy hat on his head. Even then, in shabby clothes, he had had the power to turn heads. Why, he had even charmed Aunt Ellen, who didn't as a general rule take in paying guests on a more permanent basis.

That initial hesitation on Aunt Ellen's part hadn't stopped him, she reminded herself acidly, from persevering and eventually getting his feet firmly under the large kitchen table; and keeping them there, off and on, for all these years.

'You were an administrative assistant then, in the small regional branch of that large company you still work for,' Aunt Ellen went on, pausing dreamily over her pies, 'and Sam was working on a building site, only just beginning to attract notice in the local country and western clubs where he sang in his spare time.'

'Mmm,' Roz murmured noncommittally, wishing that she could change the subject without upsetting the older woman.

'You were always such good friends with him,' her aunt went on relentlessly, obviously in full flow and thoroughly enjoying reminiscing, 'right from the start. You spent hours together, making plans for your separate and very different careers . . . '

'Let me help you with those.' Roz jumped up and, leaving her soup — that had somehow lost its delicious flavour — cooling in the bowl, she began to carry the tray of pies across to the Aga.

She found herself praying that the whole subject would be dropped, though she knew by now that it would make no difference if it was. Memories, once evoked, had a habit of staying stubbornly in your head, no matter how much you wished them gone.

Aunt Ellen had gone on to mixing up the ingredients for a fruit cake, weighing and stirring. Her hands were as busy as the tongue that chattered on happily, but Roz no longer heard the words: she had given up the fight and was conjuring up her own memories.

There had always been an attraction between Sam and her younger self, she acknowledged reluctantly. An awareness that drew them together, no matter how determined they were to stay apart. Eventually, they had indulged in a mild flirtation, knowing full well that it could come to nothing because a relationship at that time, in both of their lives, would only hinder the plans they each had for the future.

Roz had been determined, even then, to make her mark in the world of human resources management — just as Sam had been determined to find success as a singer of country music. They knew they'd be quite happy to go their own ways when the time came to move on — and up.

They would have known each other for a year or so, Roz recalled, when they had both happened to return to Aunt Ellen's for a long weekend at the same time. Their careers had been moving steadily in the right directions — but, as they confessed to each other in a quiet moment, all was not as simple as it should have been.

'I'd be quite happy,' Roz had confessed, 'especially now I've managed to get the transfer to London — which is where I've always planned to be — if it wasn't for Aunt Ellen.' She sighed. 'Oh, I know she tries to hide it, but she's worrying herself into an early grave in case concentrating on my career means I'll miss my chance when it comes to 'true love',' Roz indicated the little quote marks with her fingers, 'and get left 'all alone' the way she was when her Harry died. She won't be happy until she sees me safely settled with a husband and family.' She grimaced and shrugged. 'I'm afraid she'll have a very long wait, because I don't want that at all. I have a lot of living to do before I settle down — if indeed I ever do.'

'It's not what I want, either,' Sam confided, 'this business is far too chancy for me to think about settling down, even if I wanted to. Which I don't, of course,' he added hastily, going on, 'but the local press — when they do take an interest — won't leave my private life alone. Their constant speculating about my love life is getting me down. They're forever marrying me off to this singer or that one, and even the few fans I have think I'm fair game because I'm single. You wouldn't believe some of the offers I get after a show — some of those women have absolutely no shame.'

He looked so horrified that Roz couldn't help laughing, and then he looked so wounded by her lack of understanding that she laughed even harder. She put a careless arm round his waist, and gave him a friendly hug, in an effort to show him that she really did understand, even if it didn't seem that way.

'I know it's not really funny.' She leaned against him and continued, 'Everyone seems to be obsessed with relationships, don't they? Aunt Ellen, because she missed out on her own 'happy ever after'; the press, because romance sells newspapers; the fans, because they see any celebrity — minor or otherwise — as fair game, especially if they're unattached. It's a problem, all right.'

They were sitting on Aunt Ellen's back porch at the time, with the scent of honeysuckle all around, completely in sympathy with each other's feelings.

'It is,' Sam agreed wholeheartedly. 'I'm hardly worthy of this interest locally, and nobody's heard of me outside of the area. It's not that I don't appreciate the attention I've been getting — I do, and I know that without it I'd still be a complete nobody — but still, a little less of the poking into my personal life would be appreciated.'

'And Aunt Ellen only wants what she thinks is best for me. I do try to understand that she just worries about what will happen to me when she's gone,' Roz was quick to defend, 'but, as you say, it would be nice just to be able to please ourselves without any outside interference. It's not much to ask, and I definitely wouldn't ever marry to please anyone but myself.'

Roz lapsed into a moody silence, barely noting the sudden stillness in the young man beside her as she mused on the unfairness of it all. She did want to please her aunt, and it wasn't her intention to cause her unnecessary worry, but in this . . .

'Would you get *engaged* to please anyone but yourself?' Sam's voice sounded strange, its deep timbre holding a hesitant, almost fearful note.

'*What?*'

Roz didn't really believe what she was hearing, nor did she quite understand it. She didn't jump up, or get excited, but sat there with her arm still draped casually around Sam's waist, and waited for him to repeat himself.

'You said you wouldn't *marry* to please anyone but yourself,' he reminded her patiently, 'but would you get *engaged*?'

'Why on earth would I want to do that?'

Sam sounded inordinately pleased with himself as he went on to explain,

'It's the perfect solution, Roz. If we get engaged to each other, it lets us right off the hook. Don't you see?'

She began to. Believing him to be engaged, the local press might just stop inventing love affairs for the handsome country singer that people were beginning to notice, the fans would surely give up pursuing him so ardently, and — Roz had a sudden picture of Aunt Ellen's delighted and relieved face. If she had needed persuading at all, *that* was the deciding factor.

It was Aunt Ellen's face hovering over her that brought Roz abruptly back to the present, and she looked up, startled, into the lined and much-loved features of the woman who had been the only family she'd had since she was just a small child. She had never truly counted Sam as family, she realised, despite the 'engagement'. They had only ever been friends — good friends, certainly, but nothing more — and that was all they ever would be.

'You were miles away, dear. I asked if

you wanted a cup of tea. I'm sure Sam could do with one.'

'Mmm.' Roz gave herself a brisk mental shake before offering, 'I'll make it. I won't have you waiting on me or Sam. We're quite able to pull our own weight, and to be of help to you while we're here.'

'I remember . . . '

Aunt Ellen was off again, Roz realised ruefully, as she busied herself filling the kettle and setting out the cups, listening with only half an ear to what the older woman was saying.

' . . . that cup of tea. Do you?' The bright face turned towards Roz, the smile widening at the recollection. 'The night you and Sam announced your engagement. It tasted every bit as good as champagne to me, that cup of tea did. You could have knocked me down with a feather, when the two of you came strolling in that back door, and yet — in a funny kind of way, you know, it wasn't totally unexpected.'

Roz remembered, of course she did;

and she recalled with painful clarity the expression of total joy on her great-aunt's face, and exactly how awful it had made her feel to know that it was all nothing but a sham. By then, of course, it was far too late to change their minds and come clean even if they had wanted to, and as time went on Roz eventually even forgot to feel guilty about it.

The engagement had, after all, served its purpose. Everyone had eventually lost interest in their 'long-standing affair' — as the press referred to it on the rare occasion it was ever mentioned anymore — years before, just as Sam had so accurately predicted. He insisted he was propositioned less and less, and Aunt Ellen appeared quite happy to accept that her great-niece would eventually be ready to settle down and marry her best-loved lodger 'one day'.

She had got complacent. Roz could see that so clearly now that it was too late. She had settled into the comfortable 'engagement' to a man who, after all, had gone on to spend so much time travelling, either up and down the country or abroad, that she rarely saw him. They met up now and again in random places, just to keep the story going, but they rarely made the papers — even locally — anymore. But then they had always been quite careful not to draw attention to their regular visits to Brankstone, mindful of protecting themselves — and Aunt Ellen, of course — from unwanted publicity.

Roz sighed deeply. No wonder Aunt Ellen and everyone else was so taken in. Sometimes she had almost come to believe in it herself; though she had always known, just as Sam must have, that it would have to end some day. As a proper relationship, it was a nonstarter, and going nowhere.

Yes, it was high time they put a stop to this nonsense, once and for all. The only question was — how to do it with the minimum of fuss and upset?

# 6

Roz had no idea how long she had been standing there, hands idle, while the tea stewed in the pot, or exactly when she became aware that Sam was standing by the door watching her. It was the slight prickling of her scalp at first, and the gooseflesh rising on her arms, that warned her. She felt a flush heat her cheeks long before she turned to face him.

The look that she surprised in his eyes made the blush deepen to crimson, but it was so brief and quickly hidden that Roz couldn't be sure that she had identified it correctly. She had to fiddle with the cups to hide her confusion, and give herself time to collect her scattered wits.

'Oh, for goodness sake,' Aunt Ellen looked up from the sponge she was beating, her face a picture of consternation, 'here's Sam, gasping for that cup of tea, Rosalind. Isn't it ready yet?'

'I was just going to pour it,' she said snappily, and then was immediately ashamed. No matter what happened, she mustn't take it out on the one person who was totally innocent of any duplicity. She added, in a milder tone, 'It won't hurt him to wait.'

He came to stand beside her, ostensibly to collect his cup, but Roz was sure that he was doing it purposely to unnerve her. He was so close that she could feel the warmth of his breath on the exposed skin of her neck, and for the first time since she'd had it cut she found herself wishing that her hair were long again.

When she breathed in, she could smell a tantalising hint of spicy cologne. That, combined with the heady aroma of good honest sweat, tickled her nostrils so that she had to fight the urge to inhale deeply and savour it. Such a working-class odour would be regarded with horror in the City, she knew; and yet for some reason she found it erotic in the extreme.

How the tea found its way into the cups was a mystery to Roz. She somehow managed to pass a cup to Sam with a surprisingly steady hand, only to ruin the effect when his fingers brushed against hers — purposely, she was sure — as he took it, and then quite a large amount of the brew found its way into the saucer.

She succeeded in ignoring that quite successfully, but not the smile that told her he had noticed, and was well aware of the reason for her clumsiness. Flustered by his perception, Roz hurried a cup across to her aunt, staying on that side of the room, well away from Sam and those knowing tawny eyes.

'Your tea's getting cold, shall I pass it over?'

Roz avoided his gaze. 'I'll drink it in a while,' she said shortly; and then, in a very different tone, asked her aunt, 'Is there anything I can do for you? Peel potatoes, prepare the veg — anything at all?'

'Presently, dear,' Ellen said absently, whipping cream with an old-fashioned whisk and an energy that belied her age and skinny arms.

'Come and see what I've been doing,' Sam offered. 'You'll be quite surprised.'

And that, she told herself sternly, was just what she didn't want, any more of his surprises. She'd had more than enough for one day.

'There's plenty for me to do in here,' she told him primly. 'I can start by loading these things into the dish-washer.'

She picked up a couple of utensils, only to have them snatched away by an irate Ellen who scolded, 'I haven't finished with those yet, dear. You go along and see what Sam wants. You can help me later.'

Sam walked to the door and held it open with a grin on his face almost as wide as the door frame. To Roz's fury, she knew she had no choice but to go with him, or bring her hostility toward him right out into the open.

The minute the door had closed behind them, she turned on him with a ferocity that took him unawares and caused him to take a surprised step back, much to her own satisfaction.

'All right,' she hissed, 'you've got me out here — for what purpose, I can't imagine — but I'm warning you here and now, just don't start anything. Do you hear?'

He recovered with surprising ease, and put out his hands in a gesture of denial. 'Nothing was further from my mind,' he said innocently. 'I only thought we should finish our little talk. Decide what, if anything, we are going to do.'

'No more little tricks?' She didn't try to hide the suspicion in her tone.

'Tricks?'

'Like practicing your kissing technique on me.' She began to walk along the garden path so that the high colour of her cheeks wouldn't be apparent to him. 'I have a boyfriend who kisses very adequately, and so don't feel a pressing desire to sample your dubious expertise in the matter any further.'

'Are you quite sure?'

'Oh, stop it!' She rounded on him again. 'Look, I know we have a problem, and I'm perfectly willing to discuss it.' Her shrill tone jarred on her own ears, and she lowered it carefully to a more acceptable level, before continuing more calmly, 'What I don't need, Sam, is for you to complicate things for me any more than they are already. I was sure enough of my feelings before I came down here, and when this is over — which can't be soon enough for me — I just want you to leave me alone to live my life the way I want, with whoever I like. Is that quite clear?'

'As crystal.'

He didn't look a bit put out, she couldn't help noticing, and she felt sure she heard him mutter *Adequately* in an amused tone as he walked away — but, of course, she couldn't be absolutely sure that she wasn't mistaken, and she didn't know what it meant anyway.

Roz was suitably impressed with the amount of work Sam had managed to get done in the large garden, but she would have died before she told him so. He was already quite full enough of himself, she decided crossly, and didn't need one more person to tell him how wonderful he was, or he'd be quite unbearable.

She had to force herself to ignore a little voice that tried to insist that Sam was the least big-headed person of anyone she knew. The acclaim that had been heaped on him in country and western circles in recent months had not changed him one bit from the regular guy he had always been.

She hurried to catch Sam up, and rounded a bend in the path just in time to see him disappear into the darkened bowels of the old shed that housed the garden tools.

Peering into the gloom, she said hopefully, 'I don't suppose you'd consider being the one to break it off?'

He was suddenly, disconcertingly, right in front of her, and he gave her a very straight look from those expressive eyes, before saying, 'And be known as the singer who dumped his 'long-time lover' when he found a bit of fame and fortune? Wouldn't do much for my image, would it?'

Roz became impatient, even though she could see his point, and she huffed peevishly, 'Ooh. Since when have you cared about your 'image'? It would only be a five-minute wonder, after all.'

'It would still make all the papers,' he reminded her, 'and Andrew — is that his name? — might not take too kindly to seeing your name splashed all over the papers as the girl Sam Lawrence dumped.' Sam went to turn away, and then paused and looked at her hard. 'I suppose he does know about us?'

Roz did have the grace to blush, as she muttered, 'Well, I'm not absolutely sure . . . Like most of my associates, Andrew never reads the tabloids or glossies. You and I haven't made the press together for quite some time, and I suppose — with my hair cut — I do look quite different. I don't think *anybody* I know has any idea.'

Sam's tone was incredulous. 'You haven't told him have you? But why wouldn't you share something like that? You intend to marry the guy, so you shouldn't be keeping secrets.'

He was right. She knew it, but it only served to make her more furious, and she yelled, 'Don't you tell me what I should or shouldn't be doing. How *can* I tell him? He'd never understand. How could he, when I don't really understand it anymore myself?

'This was *your* idea, Sam. You got us into this engagement, and now you can damn well get us out. Do you hear me?'

'Loud and clear — along with half the neighbourhood, I expect.' He sighed and seemed to capitulate, suddenly becoming more reasonable. 'Look, I need some time. All I ask is that you just go along with it for just a little longer. There is a solution to this, I'm sure — I just haven't come up with it yet — but I will, Roz, trust me.'

She almost said that she'd sooner put her trust in a rattlesnake, but a grain of common sense held her back and reminded her that continually battling with Sam wasn't going to solve a single thing. Falling out with him might simply make him turn stubborn, which could make things even more awkward than they were already.

It wasn't going to help either of them in their chosen careers if they were shown in a bad light. It might soon become yesterday's news, but mud had a nasty habit of sticking, and Roz had an uncomfortable feeling that Andrew wouldn't like getting the least bit dirty, not even for her.

'I don't have much choice, do I?'

She knew she sounded ungracious, but she was more shaken that she cared to admit. She had finally been forced to face the unpleasant fact that Sam was right, and he had been all along. There really was no easy way out of their 'engagement', after all.

'Good girl.'

'You don't have to sound so pleased.'

'I'm sorry, I don't mean to. I just know that together we can work things out with the minimum of fuss. We've been engaged for almost six years, we can hardly turn our backs on it in six minutes flat, can we?'

He sounded so reasonable that she couldn't do anything but agree; and, leaving him to service Aunt Ellen's old mower in peace, Roz wandered thoughtfully back to the house, trying to analyse how she felt as she went.

She was lifting her hand to push open the back door, when the ruby-and-diamond ring — that only appeared on her left hand when she was at home — was suddenly caught in a beam of bright spring sunlight. She found herself staring at the stones, the diamonds flashing brilliant fire on her finger, and was suddenly unaccountably glad that she didn't actually have to return the lovely ring

she and Sam had chosen together —
not yet.

Of course, that was just because she
was fond of the ring, she told herself
firmly. It had nothing to do with the
man who had given it to her — nothing
at all.

# 7

The days passed pleasantly, but far too uneventfully for Roz's peace of mind, when she suddenly realised that the best part of the first week was almost over and not so much as a single hint had been dropped about the end of the engagement being imminent.

In fact, she seemed to have allowed herself to settle far too easily into a holiday mood, and with Sam and Ellen's encouragement had been quite happy to shop, sight-see, help in the house or potter in the garden.

'How long are you taking off?' she finally asked Sam, sure that he'd want to get back to the recording studio and his latest album, as time was money in his case.

'As long as it takes,' he said obliquely, which she took to mean the announcement of their parting, and made her wonder even more when he was going to come up with the plan he had promised for making it easy.

She should tackle him, she knew, and ask him outright what exactly he meant to do about it all. But it just seemed such a shame to upset the status quo when they were getting along so well. Aunt Ellen was so obviously happy having them both there. She had made no further mention about them naming the day, so it was somehow a lot easier to let things drift for a while, to simply enjoy the break from what Roz found herself reluctantly — and surprisingly — admitting was sometimes a tedious, not to mention arduous, climb up the promotion ladder.

There was a bit of a minor scare mid-week, when Aunt Ellen greeted them at breakfast one morning with the news that she had received a mysterious phone call.

'Someone asking if Sam Lawrence, the singer, lived here,' she told them worriedly. 'I told him, quite sharply, that I'd never heard of a Sam Lawrence — singer or otherwise — but if it was a reporter, he wouldn't be so easily put off.'

'Probably just a fan,' Sam assured her carelessly, but Roz didn't miss the sudden tension in his face, or the alert expression in his eyes.

'Is it anything to worry about?' Roz carefully waited until her aunt had popped in to visit Win before she voiced her query.

He sighed deeply. 'Perhaps not, but it might pay us to be a little more aware. I've had wind of an award that might be coming my way, in which case the whole media circus could start all over again any time — especially if we're seen together.'

He didn't say any more; he didn't have to. It had been a while since the papers had paid them much in the way of attention, but they both knew that, with Sam's star on the rise, their luck as far as the media was concerned could be running out.

This was the opening that Roz had been looking for, and yet she was strangely reluctant to force an issue that was beginning, more and more, to take a back seat — ridiculous as it seemed in view of it being the reason that they had come to Dorset in the first place. She couldn't even understand her own reticence, and couldn't account at all for Sam's.

Well, this is totally absurd, she told herself crossly. It can't go on indefinitely. One of us is going to have to make a move in the right direction, so I suppose it had just as well be me.

She took a deep, steadying breath, and then told him, quite firmly, 'That 'end of engagement' announcement is going to have to be decided upon and made, Sam. You know as well as I do that it can't be put off indefinitely.'

For a minute he looked startled — almost, she thought fancifully, as if he had completely forgotten the reason for them being together — and then collected himself and smiled, so that she was at once reassured.

'You're quite right. There is no easy way to do this — I'm not even sure why I thought there was. We'll set the wheels in motion, and together we'll start with telling Ellen. It's only right that she be the first to know.'

The very thought of the distress it would cause her great-aunt made Roz blanch, and very nearly tell him to leave it for a while longer. Common sense came to the rescue, and pointed out that she would only be delaying the inevitable.

'I had it in my mind,' Sam went on, 'to take Ellen, and maybe Win, too, out for a nice meal, perhaps to one of those good hotels, on the clifftop with a sea view.'

'Oh, she'd like that,' Roz enthused, and then stared at him. 'You weren't thinking of breaking it to her over dinner, were you?'

He looked sheepish, and then grinned. 'I was going to ask if you minded delaying the telling until after the evening out — if you don't mind waiting a little longer, that is?'

Roz was filled with a relief that made her light-headed and quite giddy, but she told herself firmly that it was purely concern for her great-aunt that had caused it.

'I don't mind at all,' she assured him; and then, realising it might sound as if she wasn't bothered by yet another delay, she added, 'After all, we don't want to ruin the evening for her. Just so long as I know that it will be dealt with by the time I go back to London.'

She didn't call the City 'home', and she didn't mention Andrew, but neither of them appeared to notice.

'I'll make a cup of tea, shall I?' Sam offered, and Roz sat back to enjoy the sight of him bustling around Ellen's big kitchen, setting out tea things as if he'd been born to it.

Things had been so much better between them in the last few days, and Roz was as comfortable in his company as she had ever been. There were occasional flashes of awareness, when for an instant he became almost an attractive stranger to her, but on the whole she felt that they had put their relationship back onto a proper footing.

The thought of the kiss they had shared could have caused her some concern if she let it, but she was determined to put it down to nothing more than a normal, healthy attraction between two old friends. As she reminded herself, they had shared enough kisses in the past to know that they were nothing more than a moment's careless pleasure, and no big deal at all.

'And after Ellen is told . . . ' she prompted eventually. 'What then?'

He sipped his tea thoughtfully before he spoke. 'I'm being interviewed on BBC Solent Radio at the end of next week,' he told her. 'I thought I might just drop into the conversation the fact that we've grown apart, and have mutually decided to go our separate ways in order to each concentrate on our own careers.'

'Just like that?'

'I'd have thought that the more casually it was done, the less attention it would be given — and that *is* what you want, isn't it? Less chance of lover-boy finding out, especially as the press don't seem to have managed to get any recent photos of you thus far.'

The dig about Andrew was the only one he had offered recently, so Roz allowed it to pass without comment, only saying quite mildly, 'If you think that's best.'

'Have you any better suggestions? It is the truth, after all.'

'Yes, I suppose it is.'

Better than telling the whole world that it had been little more than a hoax that had gone on for too long? Better than letting it be known that she was the one who had done the dumping, or allowing Sam to take all the blame? Yes, she supposed that it was better than any alternative that she could come up with.

She stared moodily into her cup, and found herself wondering if she would still be finishing the relationship if it had any basis in fact. If the ring on her finger had been put there with love, would she have found the strength to give it back easily?

Roz shrugged dismissively. There was no point in 'what if's, because she had never loved Sam, and he had never loved her. If he had, she would never . . .

'What are you thinking?'

The question, asked so suddenly, made her jump and flush guiltily, and she had a horrible suspicion that he was able to read her mind — which was totally ridiculous, as she was quick to remind herself. Thankfully, she was saved from having to answer by the return of Aunt Ellen.

Now that Roz was getting what she wanted, she discovered that she was quite unreasonably annoyed by Sam's unexpected capitulation. He had been so set on keeping the engagement going, had almost blackmailed her into coming home; had been difficult and unhelpful at the beginning, only to suddenly perform a complete about-turn and do exactly what she had asked him to from the start. It didn't make sense — and nor did the way she felt about it.

As the weekend approached, with her aunt getting more and more excited by the promised outing, Roz found that she was getting more and more confused about her own feelings.

Instead of being pleased that she was about to be freed from a commitment that had long since outgrown its usefulness, she found that she was dreading the final break. She was beginning to store up every minute that she spent in Sam's company in a memory bank that held many moments from their shared past.

To make matters worse, she was also beginning to remember, in far too much detail, the kiss they had recently shared. Reliving it over and over in her mind was making it take on all the proportions of a major love scene, and she found that she was looking at Sam with a new and intense awareness.

It's because he's a presentable man, she assured herself with monotonous regularity, not to mention the only one in your immediate vicinity. In London, he would only be one of many, and not half so noticeable or so inviting; but when she found herself becoming almost as excited as Aunt Ellen at the thought of going out to dinner with him, even in company, she decided that something had to be done.

The something she decided on was something that she realised she should have done very much sooner, and that was to ring Andrew. She doubted very much if *he* had taken the time to contact *her*. On reflection, that was probably just as well, because her mobile phone and laptop hadn't seen the light of day since she'd arrived in Brankstone and become immediately embroiled in the whole engagement-ending saga. Then she had simply found herself enjoying the break without the continuous interruptions that were normally accepted as part and parcel of her life. Calls and emails had simply been left unchecked — which would have been unheard-of in London.

Anyway, as she reminded herself, she was on holiday from work, and she and Andrew had sensibly agreed before she came away not to bother with phone calls. Two weeks apart was nothing, after all, when they had their whole lives together mapped out in front of them. However, it did still rankle — just a little — that ringing her anyway wouldn't have occurred to Andrew. He wasn't the most spontaneous of men. But perhaps that was something she could change.

She would invite him down to stay next weekend, she decided, and let Aunt Ellen meet him. The break together would do them both good, and she and Sam would have safely broken the news of the natural demise of the engagement to her aunt by then. Roz was sure she would be only too pleased and relieved to know, not only that Roz had someone else in her life, but that marriage in the near future was very definitely on the cards.

She waited until Saturday morning, when Sam had taken her aunt to the cash-and-carry and she had the house to herself with no fear of interruption. It would be a good time for Andrew, too, because it was the one day that he could usually be found at home relaxing after a hectic week in the office.

Unwilling to unearth her own mobile and feel obliged to start answering missed calls and texts, she lifted the receiver of her aunt's old-fashioned house phone, carefully dialled the number, and found herself feeling unaccountably nervous as she waited for Andrew to answer. She could picture his vibrating mobile phone, the very latest and most expensive must-have piece of technology, sitting on the smoked glass and chrome table in the modern, minimalistic dockside apartment, and see him sitting beside it surrounded by all the day's financial newspapers.

'Hello, Reynolds speaking.'

Roz physically jumped at the barking tone, and had to fight an urge to replace the receiver without saying a word.

'It's me, Andrew,' she began apologetically, and rushed on: 'Now, I know we decided we wouldn't ring, but . . . '

'Rosalind, darling — how lovely to hear from you.'

She couldn't help it — she held the phone away from her ear and stared at it in stunned surprise, before placing it back to her ear with a pleased smile.

'Well, I wanted to hear your voice,' she explained, more confidently, 'and hoped you wouldn't mind the interruption too much.'

'Always got time for you, my sweet,

you should know that. But tell me, when are you coming home? I miss you.'

'Do you?' Roz was thrilled, and felt a warm glow at his words. He'd never been a demonstrative man, and she was becoming quite used to his abrupt manner, but it was nice to be told, once in a while, that you were special and your absence had been noticed.

'Of course I do. You know what it's like here without a partner. After all — ' He gave a short laugh. ' — no-one wants an odd number at their dinner table, do they?'

Roz felt as if she had been slapped, but then she struggled to be sensible, to remind herself that it was just his way and she was being too sensitive. He had chosen her as his life partner, hadn't he? That had to count for something.

'I promised to stay two weeks,' she reminded him, and then went on tentatively, 'I was wondering whether you could find the time to come here — perhaps next weekend? Then we could travel back together. After all,' she rushed on, determined to have her say, 'if we're to be married, Andrew, you really should meet my great-aunt Ellen, and I know she'd just love to meet you.'

Perhaps that last statement was stretching the truth just a fraction, but Roz was well pleased with the way it sounded. She could almost see Andrew charming her aunt with his keen wit and clever conversation. How could she fail to be impressed?

'Me? Come down *there*?' The derisive laughter grated on her ear, and Roz found herself frowning as he went on, 'Me — in the heart of Dorset? I don't think so, my sweet. All that clean air . . . dear God, the very thought makes me shudder.'

Disappointment made her edgy, and she found herself snapping, 'It would only be for a day or two, Andrew. I really don't think that's so much to ask.'

'Of course it wouldn't normally, darling . . . ' His tone acquired a cajoling note. ' . . . and I would willingly do it for you — if it were any other time, much as I detest too much sea air — but this coming week is one of my busiest, with important meetings almost every day, and you know I must have my weekends to unwind, or I simply couldn't cope.'

Roz didn't even bother to point out that he could do his 'unwinding' just as well in her company. She told herself that she should have realised that she was laying herself wide open for rejection, knowing, as she did only too well, that Andrew didn't believe that a world existed outside of London. She had thought until very recently that she felt just the same, and wondered what had changed in so short a time.

They spoke for a while longer, or Andrew did, promising tickets for a show he knew that she'd been longing to see, and a meal in her favourite restaurant when she returned. He was obviously trying to make up for his refusal to do as she wanted, and Roz really did try to be grateful; but his lack of understanding hurt nonetheless, and she could only feel relief when she finally replaced the receiver.

She wandered moodily round the house, trying to tell herself that everything would be all right once she was back in London again. It was too easy to forget how crazy it was there when you were away from the capital and your place of work for any length of time — and how taken up you could be with the pace of things, and the great need you felt to keep your finger firmly on the pulse.

'It will be all right. I know it will.'

She spoke the words aloud, as if doing so would give her assurance, but she also found herself wondering if Andrew would ever so much as cancel a single meeting for her, whatever the reason.

What if she were taken ill? She found herself pointlessly asking the question. What if she were in labour with their baby? What then?

For a long moment the question made her stand very still, as she wondered for the first time if Andrew even wanted a family, and she realised that it was just one of the many things they had never got round to discussing. She hadn't been at all sure that she wanted one herself until that moment, but she suddenly knew, beyond the shadow of a doubt, that she actually did.

Yes. She nodded with a firmness that surprised her. She wanted all those things that she had professed to despise in the past. She wanted the husband, the home and the family, in that order — and most of all, she acknowledged, she wanted the love to wrap it all up in. The burning question was: did Andrew want that, too — any of it?

She seemed to have been gazing out of the front room window for a very long time, staring with unseeing eyes at the now-tidy sweep of the weed-free drive. She felt vaguely disenchanted with everything about her life and was

113

filled with unusual doubts. She was actually fighting a strong desire to cry when the old estate car was swung into the drive with as much panache as if it were a Porsche.

She watched as Sam jumped from the driver's seat, performing an energetic leap across the wide bonnet before throwing open the passenger door and helping a smiling Aunt Ellen from the car. Suddenly, Roz was laughing, too, her ill-humour forgotten as she went out to help unload the shopping.

'And what have you been doing with yourself this morning?' Sam asked, dropping a casual arm round her waist and an equally careless kiss on her cheek.

Roz smiled up at him, letting the warmth of his greeting cheer her still more, as she replied carefully, 'Oh, nothing much, I'm afraid. I should have come with you and made myself useful.'

'Haven't you even put the kettle on?' Aunt Ellen chided. 'I'm spitting feathers here.'

'No sooner said than done,' Roz promised, rushing ahead, pausing only to hold the door open for Sam, who was so laden down with boxes that he could barely see over the top. She was putting the kettle to boil when he emerged from the walk-in pantry, and when she held out a hand, he whipped a packet of chocolate biscuits out from behind his back with all the flair of a magician producing a rabbit from a hat.

'Do you think you can get Ellen to have a lie-down before tonight?' he said under his breath. 'She's been on the go since first thing, and looks worn out, but is still insisting that she's just fine. She won't listen to me.'

Not many men would be so caring, even about someone as special as Aunt Ellen, Roz knew, and Sam went up one more notch in her estimation. Watching him through the open pantry door as he unloaded tins, bottles and packets very expertly, she realised that he never seemed to concern himself too much about his image, or what people might think. Sam was absolutely his own person, and she knew very well how rare that was in a man.

'I thought I'd pop into Win's later, to find out what she's wearing,' her aunt proclaimed when she finally stopped pottering, sank gratefully into a chair, and looked hopefully at the teapot.

'I wouldn't,' Roz advised, arranging the biscuits tastefully on a plate. 'She told me yesterday that she intended to have a good rest this afternoon, because she's not used to late nights, and doesn't want to disgrace herself by falling asleep at the table. She's wearing her good navy suit with the black patent accessories, if that's any help.' The latter was only an educated guess, but as it was what Win usually wore out, Roz felt quite safe making it.

Ellen looked at first taken aback, and then thoughtful. She sipped her tea in silence, but Roz was not surprised when her ploy worked, and her aunt suddenly said, 'I think I might just put my feet up for an hour — and I shall wear my royal blue dress.'

Sam gave a jubilant thumbs-up sign from the doorway of the store cupboard, accompanied by a smile and a wink that caused Roz's heart to somersault most uncomfortably.

'I've got some cooling eye-pads that you're welcome to use,' she offered, turning her attention determinedly to her aunt, 'and I can do your hair later, if you'd like. I brought my hairstyling paraphernalia with me and there'll be plenty of time.'

'Oh, would you, dear?' The older woman looked so pleased that Roz wondered why she hadn't thought to offer before, and she made herself a promise that she would ensure her aunt looked a million dollars for her evening out.

\* \* \*

The house was quiet, the lunch things all put away, and Aunt Ellen had gone quite happily to lie down on her bed.

117

Roz and Sam, with nothing else to do, made themselves comfortable in the sitting room.

'I never thought to ask — ' Roz only spoke to break the silence, and because she wouldn't let herself believe that being alone with Sam could cause her to be tongue-tied. ' — if you had actually got around to booking a table for tonight?'

He gave her a very straight look, and raised his eyebrows comically almost to his hairline, before saying in the driest tone, 'Fancy me forgetting to do that!'

'You didn't?' Then she laughed, but not as lightly as she might have wished. 'Oh, all right. I didn't really think you had forgotten — I was just checking.'

'Come and sit down,' he tugged at her hand until she sank onto the sofa beside him, 'and put your feet up. Do you want the TV on?'

She really wanted to say yes, but she was numbingly aware of the lean length of his thigh pressing against hers, and the warmth of his arm through the sleeve

118

of her silk blouse was sending tingling messages to her brain that couldn't be ignored, no matter how much she tried — and she did try, very hard.

'Uh.'

It sounded like *No*, and the television remained stubbornly off. She wanted to move away, but knew if she did he was sure to guess why, and so it was simpler to remain where she was.

'That was a master stroke of yours, telling Ellen about Win taking a nap.' Sam relaxed back against the cushions and stretched, before placing a careless arm along the back of the couch, where it brushed tantalizingly against the sensitive skin at the back of her neck and sent a shiver of awareness down her spine.

God, she felt so cross with herself. She'd been home for a week now, had known Sam for seven long years, and been 'engaged' for six of those. How was it, she asked herself furiously, that he suddenly had the power to make her feel like a gauche teenager, and he wasn't even aware of it — or her, for that matter?

'She did look a little tired.' Roz forced herself to concentrate on the idle conversation, and on relaxing muscles that were rigid with tension, ignoring with difficulty the close proximity of the man beside her.

'You looked a bit upset when we first got home.' He leaned forward, an expression of concern on his good-looking face. 'Haven't received bad news, I hope.'

She hadn't intended to say anything to anyone about her conversation with Andrew, but somehow, perhaps because he really seemed to care, she found herself telling Sam — of all people — about it.

'I had thought that I might persuade him to come down towards the end of next week. It would really round off my holiday to have him stay here for a couple of days before I leave,' she admitted, trying not to let the hurt she was feeling show in her voice. 'Then we could have travelled back together, but he's far too busy with meetings, and the paperwork they always result in, all the week. There's no way he could cancel anything; and of course,' she added loyally, 'I wouldn't expect him to.'

'Of course not.'

There was no hint of criticism in Sam's even tone, for which Roz was grateful, and she went on, 'I had thought that once you and I had told Aunt Ellen about the engagement being off, maybe then, if Andrew had been able to come — well — she would have been able to see for herself how suitable he is for me.'

The way she said it, it didn't even sound quite right to her own admittedly sensitive ears; but again, Sam just nodded as if he knew just what she meant. She should have known that he would understand.

'And you're quite sure that there's no chance of Andrew changing his mind?' he asked, his tawny gaze never wavering from her face. 'Not even if you told him how much it would mean to have him here?'

It was a reasonable enough question, but it only served to make Roz more fed up than she was already. 'I'm quite sure, Sam, but I know he would come if he could.'

'I'm sure he would come down if he was free,' Sam soothed, but even as he spoke, Roz suddenly remembered a time, years before, when she had rung him simply because she was homesick and alone in London. She recalled, all too clearly, how Sam had caught the very next train to be with her; and, rearranging his busy schedule, he had stayed until she was settled and happy to be left once more.

'Yes, he'll come when he can.'

Who was she trying to convince? she asked herself; but when Sam smiled at her like that, with a disconcertingly tender look in his eyes, she even began to wonder if it really mattered whether Andrew bothered to come and join her at all.

# 8

That Roz was really quite angry with Andrew was a fact that she only really understood and acknowledged as she soaked in a deep and soothing bubble bath.

Yes, angry, she admitted, almost in wonder. She was angry that her wishes obviously didn't count for very much in his scheme of things, and also angry — and hurt — that she clearly meant so little to him.

Was this really the man, she asked herself, who she planned to spend the rest of her life with? A man who was clearly impressed by her work ethic, but was ever willing to put her personal happiness a poor second to the flimsiest of work commitments — and even his own relaxation. How many times had he asked her to give up her own precious free time? And how many times had she gladly done so for him? Yet he seemed to be only too willing to forgo time spent in her company for anything that wasn't work related.

She stopped her train of thought quite suddenly, horrified at the bitterness she felt towards the man she had come to believe she was so completely in tune with. She refused to allow herself to remember and accept that it was Andrew's tune that they invariably danced to, and reminded herself instead of just how keen he was to get ahead, and that it was to both of their advantages that he did.

'Sometimes, in life, you have to be single-minded.' She soaped her body busily, listening to the words as they were spoken aloud, as if that would give them more emphasis — more truth. 'It does no good to be faint-hearted in the world of business when there are too many people waiting to step into your shoes.'

Roz was beginning to feel better, and

to keep the feeling going, she went on to recall all the times that Andrew had sent her flowers, the lovely jewellery he sometimes surprised her with, and the very evident pride he always took in her appearance.

It *almost* worked, she was beginning to feel good about him again, and to forgive him for not being just what — and where — she wanted when she needed him . . . until she realised just what she was doing.

She rose from the water impatiently, splashing the floor in her haste and annoyance, saying crossly, 'You're just making excuses for him,' and knowing that she really was doing just that made her angry all over again.

The towel was applied with such vigour that her skin positively glowed, and she knew that, for two pins she would ring Andrew again, with no consideration for his precious rest and relaxation, and tell him just what she thought of him.

How can you be *grateful*, she asked

herself, for flowers and jewellery that were probably chosen by a secretary on his instruction? How could he do other than compliment you on your appearance, when he practically tells you what to wear?

Into her mind, sneakily, crept the memory of the time one spring when she had been very run-down after a bad bout of 'flu. Sam had appeared from nowhere, wrapped her up warmly, and driven her miles into the country, just because she had happened to mention that she was very fond of primroses. He had found them, too, and the sight of them growing wild had lifted her spirits far more than the delivery of an expensive bouquet would have done. When she had asked him why he'd gone to so much trouble, he'd said that it was worth it to see her smile.

*He has more spare time than Andrew*, she reminded herself; but she knew as she did so that it was just an excuse. She was becoming more and more uncomfortable with the turn her thoughts were taking, but it didn't help at all when she realised that, though the engagement ring was the only jewellery that Sam had ever given her, she much preferred that one piece they had chosen together to all the more showy trinkets that Andrew had presented her with.

Even as Roz was dressing, taking infinite care and attention to detail, she knew that if she was wise she would not go out in Sam's company that night. In her vulnerable state, she was far too susceptible to Sam's special brand of charm. She was very aware that any more dalliances like the one in the garden could cause her to make more unfavourable comparisons between the two men in her life, and question her carefully laid plans for the future into the bargain, if she wasn't very careful.

'Oh, for heaven's sake.' She outlined her lips with a surprisingly steady hand. 'Aren't you being a little overdramatic, Rosalind Blake? There is just no comparison you can make between those two men. Andrew, for all his faults, is a City gent, with all the qualities that you've ever looked for in a husband — a man who totally under-stands your ambitions and the life you wish to lead. Sam — well — Sam is Sam, and you've known him for far too long to have your head turned by his admitted charm or by his handsome face — ' She paused for breath, before reminding herself in the firmest tone: ' — and besides, you can't possibly let Aunt Ellen or Win down like that.'

She didn't bother to add that she deserved an outing, if only to make up for the disappointment she had suffered at Andrew's hands that day; but the thought was there, right in the forefront of her mind — and, more uncomfort-ably, the rejoinder surfaced that it would just serve Andrew right if she ended the evening in Sam's very warm, and sometimes tempting, arms.

★ ★ ★

'There.' Roz gave a final, satisfied pat to her aunt's — for once — tamed and neatly-set hair.

'Oh . . . ' Ellen twisted this way and that before the mirror. ' . . . don't I look nice? You *have* done a lovely job. Win will be that put out,' she added, in such a satisfied tone that Roz chanced a little grin behind the blue-clad back.

'You're really looking forward to this, aren't you?' She brushed a silver hair from the sleeve of the older woman's dress and smiled at her fondly.

'I am.' Her aunt positively beamed. 'It's such a treat for us to be going out with you two. I know we go out with our club from time to time, but they're all old biddies like us. It's much more exciting to have Sam take us out.'

'Who's an old biddy?' Sam put his head round the door, and looked from one to the other. 'I don't see any.' He winked at Roz and asked, 'Who's the babe with the posh hairdo? Don't I get an introduction?'

Aunt Ellen twirled a little awkwardly, on shoes that were a touch too high for her, but managed to spread the pleats of her skirt quite satisfactorily. 'Don't I look lovely?'

'So modest, too!' He laughed, and planted a smacking kiss on the wrinkled cheek, before putting a careless arm around each of them and saying in all seriousness, 'You look gorgeous, Ellen; and — ' He turned to Roz, his voice deepening. ' — so do you.'

It was just a silly compliment, nothing at all to get excited about, but her heart wouldn't listen, and its beat accelerated until she was quite breathless. She knew, then, exactly why she had spent too much time and effort on getting ready, and why it was suddenly worth it.

The two women stood for a moment in the shelter of Sam's arms. They were all smiling, and it seemed to Roz as if that was how they belonged, in the tight circle that made them almost closer than just family. Then they separated, and she had to suppress a shiver.

*Fanciful*, she chided herself, and skipped off upstairs to fetch her jacket, with a brief 'Won't be long!' flung over her shoulder.

She wasted long minutes in front of the mirror waiting for the hectic flush on her cheeks to die down, and for the sparkle in her eyes to dim. It seemed ridiculous to be so full of anticipation about a simple meal in a local hotel with people she had known for years, when she spent a great deal of her time in London helping to entertain clients in some of the best restaurants in the city.

She checked her appearance for the umpteenth time, unable to resist that one last look before she left the room.

Had she tried too hard? Would Sam think her too sophisticated? He had seemed to like the way she looked when she was downstairs. She scowled at her reflection, and then narrowed her green eyes and tried to see herself as he might have done.

She always tried to look her best, she reminded herself. There was no reason at all for tonight to be different, and she owed it to her aunt and Win to make an extra effort to match the trouble they had gone to in looking good for the evening. She mustn't let the side down.

But was the silk suit too dressy, the green too green, the straight skirt too short, and the matching accessories simply too much?

In the end, Roz lost all patience with herself — *and about time, too,* she fumed — wondering what on earth was the matter with her. She wore the suit all the time in London, for heaven's sake. It always made her feel good, bringing out the red in her hair as it did, plus the green of her eyes. It was comfortable, it was elegant, and if Sam didn't like it — tough. And why was she worried about what he liked, anyway? Roz picked up her bag at last, and went downstairs.

'About time, too.' Aunt Ellen turned

from the mirror and gave her hair one last pat. 'I thought you must have decided to change, or something.'

'Why?' Roz couldn't keep the agitation from her tone. 'Don't I look all right in this? Do you think I *should* change?'

'I think you look absolutely charming. It's a beautiful suit. I noticed — ' She gave a delighted chuckle. ' — that Sam couldn't keep his eyes off you, even after all the time you've known each other.'

'He couldn't?' Roz didn't even try to ignore the warm glow that the words gave her, but then she looked round and asked, 'Where is he anyway?'

'Oh, he went round to fetch Win, so now that you're finally here, we'd just as well go on out.' Her aunt reached for her cashmere shawl, and Roz helped to tuck it around her shoulders. 'It's at times like this,' she confided, 'that I do wish I had a better car. It's fine for the cash-and-carry, but I just hope that Sam has given those seats a good clean.'

Laughing, they went outside arm-in-arm to find Sam waiting by the front door; resplendent, Roz noticed belatedly, in an unfamiliar dark suit, and — unheard-of for him — a collar and tie.

'Where's your cap, chauffeur?' She grinned, and then gaped at the sight of the limousine parked in the place of the old estate car, dropping her jaw still more at the real live uniformed chauffeur holding the rear door open. 'Oh, my God, is that a Mercedes, and is that really a chauffeur?'

Aunt Ellen recovered first, sweeping into the luxury car to the manner born, and settling herself, regally erect, beside a still faintly-stunned and overawed Win.

'I'm impressed,' Roz whispered, as she, too, prepared to glide forward.

Sam grinned, and she caught a tantalizing hint of cologne as he leaned toward her and, close to her ear, breathed, 'So am I,' his gaze lingering over the shimmering green of her suit.

Inside the car, the two older women had found their tongues with a vengeance, and they chattered nineteen to the dozen for the whole of the smooth ride. Roz found that her tongue actually seemed to be tied in knots, and that it was taking her all of her time to cope with a heartbeat that had begun to race out of control from the minute that Sam had taken his place on the seat close beside her.

*Ridiculous*, she told herself, as part of her itched to move away and set a safe space between them — and another, more insistent, part urged her to move closer yet, and to put her hand out to cover the tanned skin of the fingers that rested casually on the knee of the dark suit.

Roz shivered suddenly and clasped her hands tightly in her lap, jumping almost out of her seat when Sam touched her fingers and asked, 'Are you cold?'

'Who, me?'

*My God*, she asked herself, *did that*

*little, pathetic squeak really come out of my own mouth?*

'Could you turn the heater up, please?'

Sam's authoritative request made her protest, in a voice that was fractionally stronger, 'I'm not cold, really. A goose walked over my grave, that was all.'

For the rest of the short drive, Roz let the excited conversation of the two women, interspersed by comments from Sam, flow over and around her while she gave herself a severe lecture on the foolishness of letting a handsome face, and equally handsome compliments, turn her head and affect her heart. It seemed to work, and she was pleased to notice that she could accept Sam's hand as he helped her from the car without so much as a tremor in her own.

The two older women twittered and cooed like birds as they admired and approved of the hotel that Sam had chosen; and, like birds, they preened and tidied their brilliant feathers, straightening a pleat here and a fold there.

'How do we look?' they asked in unison, with a last confident pat, also in unison, of the neatly coiffured heads.

'Wonderful.' Sam took his place between them and, offering each an arm, swept them forward into the hotel foyer.

It was the right thing to do. It was the only thing to do, and Roz was quite aware of that. So, why then, she asked herself impatiently, did she immediately feel like a spare part and wish that she hadn't bothered to come? She was ashamed, and bitterly disappointed that she could be so absolutely childish.

She allowed a moment to collect herself, and then took a deep, pull-yourself-together breath before straightening her shoulders and following the laughing trio into the building with a brilliant smile pinned firmly in place.

Roz never felt left out again, not even for a moment. Sam divided himself, neatly and equally, between the three of them, and she found that she was actually enjoying herself hugely. He was funny, he was charming, and so relaxed himself that every tense knot that had been caused by the stresses of the last week unravelled, until Roz felt warm and mellow and at peace with the whole world.

The peace was rudely shattered when a young, and very pretty girl approached the table to ask for Sam's autograph. She was quite shy, and not at all pushy, but unfortunately her action aroused the curiosity of the majority of the other diners, and several of the younger ones even formed a queue.

The manager tried to intervene, and did at least make it very clear that anyone discovered using their mobile to take photographs would be asked to leave immediately, pointing out that as guests of the hotel, Sam and his party should be offered some respect and some privacy.

Sam was patience itself, taking time to speak with each person and happily signing the serviettes and menus that were waved hopefully under his nose, but in the meantime his meal went cold and the three women were pushed and jostled in the crush.

'Sorry about that,' he offered when the little crowd had at last dispersed. He shrugged helplessly. 'Somehow I didn't think that anyone would recognize me here.'

'Oh, I thought it was quite exciting, didn't you, Win?' It was easy to see that Aunt Ellen was impressed, as she added thoughtfully, 'I hadn't realised you were quite so well-known. Perhaps I'd better have a signed photo of you myself, to display in the dining room at home.'

'Ooh, and me!' Win wasn't about to be left out. 'I had no idea that you were really famous, Sam.'

He laughed uproariously at that, throwing back his head and showing even white teeth.

'Doesn't it annoy you?' Roz asked curiously, trying not to be too impressed by the easy way he handled his growing fame. 'The way those people obviously feel as if they own you, and that they have the right to your time whatever you're doing, must surely be quite intrusive.'

'It's those people, and others like them, who are putting me where I am.' His gaze held her own as he explained, 'Without them buying my CDs and paying to come to my concerts, I would still be working on a building site. I try not to lose sight of that.'

'That's nice,' she murmured, and meant it.

A pianist had been playing softly throughout the meal, and it was Aunt Ellen who noticed: 'Oh, listen, Sam, isn't that one of your songs from the CD that I have at home?' — just a second before a discreet cough drew their attention to the manager of the hotel hovering by the table.

'I hesitate to ask,' he said apologetically, 'but we have had several requests for you to sing. I realise that it's rather impertinent — and you must, of course, feel free to refuse . . . '

Aunt Ellen clapped her hands together, and Win gave a little excited squeak. Roz felt a thrill of anticipation, but she refused to add her persuasion to theirs, wanting it to be Sam's decision and his alone.

Everyone was looking their way expectantly, but Sam didn't move until he had asked each of his own guests if they minded. His own expression was carefully blank, Roz noticed, with no indication given of his own feelings; but when he rose to his feet it was with relaxed ease, and he strolled over to the pianist with the briefest smile to acknowledge the enthusiastic applause that greeted his move.

Roz realised, as she watched him chatting to the musician, that it was actually a while since she had heard him sing. Yet in the early days she had been a regular when he had sung in country and western clubs locally, dressed in shabby denims and the battered cowboy hat which had become almost his trademark, but taken nothing away from his admitted good looks.

Her aunt and Win were almost beside themselves, and twittering with excitement by the time Sam had professed his satisfaction with the music chosen, and was seated on the high stool that the obviously delighted manager had provided.

The young girl who had approached him initially left her table to sit, cross-legged and adoring, at his feet. She was immediately joined by several others of a similar age, and if Roz had still been in her teens, she knew she would have had to fight the strongest urge to do the same. She was impressed that everyone appeared to be adhering to the 'no photographs' ruling, and there wasn't a mobile to be seen

From the opening line of the first song, Sam held his small audience in the palm of his hand. Watching him, Roz was enthralled. The deep timbre of his voice rose and fell with each closely-followed note, bringing unexpected goosebumps to Roz's arms. He'd always had a good voice — but, if anything, it had improved with age and experience, and was now exceptional.

'Isn't he wonderful?' Aunt Ellen enthused, and Roz had to bite her tongue to prevent herself giving voice to the impatient *Ssh* that rose to her lips.

She sat motionless, elbows on table, chin on hands, her gaze fixed on Sam, completely carried along with the magic that he carelessly wove around his audience. She followed his every move and treasured every golden note.

The girl at his feet rose suddenly, breaking the spell for Roz. She stepped into the space beside Sam as if it were where she belonged, her pretty face tilted to one side as she stared into his eyes and took the words of the song for her own.

The sour, bitter taste of jealousy filled Roz's throat until she almost gagged. She watched as her fingers —

of their own volition, and despite the pretty bronze-painted nails — curved into vicious claws that itched to tear the smile from the girl's pale face. Reminding herself that the girl in question was little more than a besotted child didn't help.

*How dare she?* Roz raged silently. *Who does she think she is? Doesn't she know that Sam is mine? Mine. All mine.*

It took some moments, long moments, when she had to force herself to remain seated and silent — when what she wanted to do was stand up and claim him publicly as her fiancé — to get herself under some sort of control. When she had, Roz was appalled.

*What are you doing?* she demanded of herself. *What the hell do you think you are doing? He is not yours — he has never, ever, been yours. He never will be yours.*

He turned then, away from the girl, who had stepped back when she realised she no longer had his attention.

His smile was clearly for Roz — for her, and her alone. But she was determined, by then, not to let his very obvious charm affect her again, and she stared back into eyes that were shadowed by the dim lights, refusing to return his smile with one of her own.

Appreciative applause told her that the song had ended, but still Sam held her gaze, his own quite steady. She wanted to glare at him, she wanted to frown her displeasure, but knew she had no right to feel it, let alone show it. Most of all, she wanted to turn away, to raise a careless shoulder in his direction to show him that nothing he did mattered to her at all.

The song he began was one she wasn't familiar with, and she was too busy trying to wrestle her gaze from his to concentrate at first. The room was hushed; Roz was vaguely conscious of the curious looks that were beginning to come her way, and that the two older women sitting with her were looking positively gooey-eyed and smiling: soft, entranced smiles.

The song was for her. There could have been no doubt about it to anyone sitting in that hotel restaurant, nor that it was a love song written with someone special in mind.

The icy determination to ignore him began to melt as the words made sense and undermined the resolution to remain unmoved by his single-minded assault on her senses. A warmth sizzled along her veins and, watching his lips move, she was suddenly reminded of the kiss they had shared and of the special way it had made her feel.

Like someone in love . . .

Her eyes widened, and her breath caught deep in her throat. She stared at Sam as if she'd never seen him before in her life, taking in the lean strength of him, the dark good looks that were so familiar, and yet suddenly so new and frightening.

The song ended, and she watched as Sam touched one finger to his lips in a gesture so loving and so romantic that it lifted her heart on gentle wings to beat frantically in her breast. The applause was loud and enthusiastic, but Roz was conscious only of the man who made his way determinedly towards her, to lift her fingers gallantly to his lips, and smile into her eyes with a look that made her dream sweet, impossible dreams.

'Oh, that was wonderful, Sam. Wasn't that wonderful, Win?'

Roz had all but forgotten that the other women were there, and it took a real effort on her part to join in with their excited conversation. People were congratulating Sam on giving such a professional, yet totally unexpected, performance; and though he smiled and nodded, he had eyes only for Roz, and she positively glowed.

'Let's get out of here — just for a moment,' he murmured, so close to her ear that Roz could feel the warmth of his breath lifting a strand of her hair, and she shivered deliciously.

She rose from her seat immediately,

giving no thought to what was to come, but aware that whatever she was feeling, he was feeling it, too. It was there, written clearly in the tawny eyes, the golden flecks lit brighter than ever before as they encouraged her to go with him — and she knew that she would, wherever he wanted her to go.

Aunt Ellen and Win weren't so eager to leave, but were anxious to prolong their moment of glory, surrounded as they were by an admiring crowd.

Laughing, Sam took her hand, and asked the manager, in passing, to give the two women anything they wanted. 'A breath of air,' he explained, 'back in a moment. I doubt they'll even miss us.'

They were barely through the door and onto the terrace before she was drawn into his arms with a determination, and yet a gentleness that couldn't be denied — even had she wanted to do so.

She lifted her face for his kiss; her eyelids had fluttered down and her lips had parted at the first light pressure of his own, a tantalizing foretaste of what was to come.

Roz sighed, past thinking, only aware of feelings that clamoured to be recognized and a knowledge of what was surely to be . . .

Suddenly, a flashbulb popped and bathed them in brilliant light, taking them completely by surprise, before their own natural reflexes made them leap apart. It was too late: the damage had been done, and a precious moment had been ruined for them forever.

# 9

'Who's the lovely lady, Sam?'

The coarsely insinuating voice made Roz wince, and she swayed on her feet, staring at the lone photographer with bemused eyes, wondering where he had come from and what he wanted. She didn't have long to wait.

'What does your long-time fiancée think of your new lady — or doesn't she know?'

He obviously thought that she was someone else, that Sam was two-timing her. Her first instinct was to laugh in the man's face, and hot on the heels of that was the need to defend him from a spiteful insinuation that she knew to be untrue.

'I . . . ' she began furiously, only to be silenced by Sam's emphatic, 'No.'

With a speed that made her head spin, he whirled her round, and she found herself back inside the hotel without her feet ever having touched the ground.

Sam went back outside, but he was soon back, saying, 'I thought I might reason with him, but he's made himself scarce. Who called the press?' he demanded angrily of the manager who had suddenly appeared.

The man looked worried, and apologetic. 'One of the guests, one would assume — ' He frowned. ' — because I can't believe for one minute that any of my staff would behave in such a disgraceful fashion. I wouldn't have had this happen for the world, especially in view of your earlier kindness. Is there anything I can do to help? Perhaps get some of my staff to check the grounds?'

Sam laughed, but it wasn't a pleasant sound. 'It sounds like a good idea,' he conceded, 'but it was just one photographer and he'll be long gone.'

'What will happen?' Roz huddled back against the wall, terrified that someone else was about to burst in and

thrust another camera into her unsus-
pecting face.

She hadn't been photographed with
Sam for quite some time, and had
forgotten just how sneaky any member
of the media could be once they got a
hint of a story.

'I can offer you and your party
rooms,' the manager suggested. 'At this
time of year the place is never full, and
you'd be more than welcome.'

'And provide them with a whole *new*
story?' Sam asked wryly.

The man looked embarrassed, and
Roz felt herself flush as she was forced
to acknowledge the obvious conclusions
they would draw from an overnight
stay. Pointless to remind Sam that they
had two elderly ladies as chaperones,
because she was sure that would cut no
ice with a reporter determined to
present his editor with a juicy story
— especially when he had already taken
the compromising photograph he'd
come for.

'We'll have to be seen to leave, I'm

afraid.' Sam put a comforting arm around her shoulders. 'I wouldn't put you through it, but you must see that we have no choice.'

'I do see,' Roz said calmly, determined not to add to his problems by causing an unnecessary fuss, 'but we'll have to get Aunt Ellen and Win out separately so they're not involved. Having a camera thrust in their faces would frighten them both to death.'

In the end, it was all arranged very satisfactorily when one of the other restaurant guests, hearing of their dilemma, offered to drive the two elderly ladies home in his car. The ladies in question, in fact, expressed themselves quite willing to have their photographs taken, and it took Sam all his time to persuade them that it really wasn't a good idea at all. He, of all people, had quickly come to understand that to be the focus of media attention was not nearly as glamorous as it appeared to be. It could be nothing short of a nuisance at best, and an absolute plague at worst.

'It would mean the end of all my anonymous visits to you,' he told them, and that clinched their support in getting home without inviting any interest. They left without another word of protest.

When it was time for the pair of them to leave, Roz knew that she would have given anything for a wig, dark glasses, and an oversized, enveloping mackintosh. She said as much to Sam, who simply advised, 'Just keep your head down, so anyone still out there won't get a clear look at you, hold onto me, and run like hell. Don't worry — ' He managed a grin. ' — I'll do my best to get us out of this in one piece, and without too much damage done.'

It seemed he had kept his promise when the driver managed to get them safely away from the hotel and home by such a roundabout route that anyone trying to follow would quickly have been lost. But Roz was to remember those words all too clearly when she woke after a particularly restless night, to find that her face and Sam's were spread all over the tabloid newspapers for all to see. The lone photographer, it seemed, had wasted no time selling his picture.

'Oh, you did a fine job,' she accused him bitterly, thrusting one of the papers beneath his nose. 'The editors obviously recognized me, even if the photographer didn't, and now so will everyone else in the country. How could you let this happen?'

The sight of her and Sam unashamedly kissing the faces off each other on all those front pages inflamed her anger until she felt fit to burst with the unfairness of it all. The way she had felt, the fact that she had *wanted* him to kiss her, was all forgotten in the humiliating aftermath, the need to hit out, to punish — and Sam was altogether too handy a target.

'I did it on purpose — right?' he ground out, fury sending warning sparks from his eyes, except that she was too enraged herself to see them.

'What else am I supposed to think?' she spat, glaring at him. 'It was your idea to keep this damn engagement going, and now it won't only be Aunt Ellen and Win-next-door avidly waiting for a wedding announcement, will it?'

They were going at each other hammer and tongs, and the only surprising thing was that they had somehow been able to keep their anger in check until they were safely ensconced in the garden shed, well out of Aunt Ellen's hearing.

She was installed at the kitchen table with a big pair of scissors in one hand, and the damning evidence of the newspaper photos in the other, happily snipping away in an effort to fill the scrapbook she kept of Sam's cuttings. Roz found herself wishing she could only be glad that they had made someone happy, but it was an uphill struggle to find any good in what had happened.

She'd be a laughing stock. She shuddered, wondering how she would ever show her face in London again. What would her boss think? What would Andrew think? Her green eyes widened in horror, and then narrowed as she pushed her face into Sam's and said, unthinkingly and through gritted teeth, 'If this has all been an elaborate plan either for publicity or to get me to marry you . . . '

His nose was almost touching hers as he snarled, 'I don't *need* this sort of publicity — and marry *you*? I'd as soon jump off of the lifting bridge at Poole Quay on a stormy night.'

*Ooh*. Her hand positively itched to slap the sneer right off his handsome face. *Too handsome*, she told herself savagely, *for his own damn good*.

'So . . . ' Roz glowered up at him, wishing with all her heart that she were a good six inches taller and could look him right in the eye. She was sure it would have made all the difference. 'Why keep me shackled to you — against my will, I might add — when I made it patently clear that I wanted

157

out? None of this would have happened if you hadn't insisted that I come down here.'

Did he look sheepish? Roz could have sworn that for a moment there he had, but the look was so fleeting that she couldn't have been totally sure; and so, regretfully, she had to let it go instead of tackling him about it as she would have liked.

'If you wanted out so badly — ' Sam matched her, glare for furious glare. ' — why didn't you just do it? Tell me that, eh? Why come down here at all, if it wasn't what you wanted to do? You could have written to Ellen. Okay — ' He put up his hand to silence the protest she began to utter. ' — so it might have been a shock to begin with, but no doubt she'd have gotten over it eventually. Be fair — if you know how to be — you agreed with everything I said, but now it's just convenient for you to heap all the blame on my head.'

The unfairness of it quite took her

breath away, but Roz refused to allow herself to be browbeaten by words, and words that she could more than match any day of the week.

'Yes,' she hissed, placing her hands firmly onto her hips and leaning forward accusingly, 'because you're the one who's spent the past week trying to get me into a clinch at every available opportunity.'

She knew as she spoke that she was being totally unfair, but somehow she had to convince herself that she'd had no hand in bringing this disaster down onto her own head.

'Well . . . ' The expression on his face became almost smug. 'I didn't have to try very hard, did I?'

This time, Roz made no attempt to control her actions, and the flat of her hand connected, fairly and squarely, with the tanned jaw. He never moved so much as a muscle. He didn't even flinch, though the skin on her palm tingled painfully, and she noted with satisfaction that she had left the clear print of her hand sketched in crimson on his cheek.

The anger, all of it, left her quite suddenly. She had made a huge mistake in coming home, she saw it quite clearly now that it was too late, and then she had compounded it by going along with Sam's crazy scheme. She had left everything to him, trusting that he would sort it all out satisfactorily, when what she should have done was to follow her own instincts and been honest with everyone, including Aunt Ellen and even Andrew, from the start. She dreaded to think what he would make of all this, and was trying desperately most of the time not to think about it.

Sam stood, tall, silent and unmoving. She couldn't deny the awareness that sizzled between them, even now, but she was at a complete loss to try and explain it, all she did know was that she didn't want to argue with him anymore.

Slowly, she turned to go, and though he made no move to stop her, Roz was sure that she could feel his hard stare burning a hole in her back.

Her hand was on the latch. All she had to do was lift it to open the door, but something stopped her, made her turn to face him one last time and ask one last question.

'Why, Sam? Why that whole performance with the love song? What was that all about?'

It had seemed so special, so wonderful, and she had believed every word — and every long, lingering look — and now she couldn't walk away until she knew the truth.

His expression hardened, and his tone was even harder, as he told her, 'You just answered your own question, didn't you? It was a performance — and the audience absolutely loved it.' Having said his piece, his mouth clamped shut in a straight and uncompromising line.

'But why use me?' It was little more than a whisper.

Sam shifted uneasily, but his tone

was quite steady, and as reasonable as his explanation. 'I had to get rid of the girl, didn't I? She was looking set to make a nuisance of herself. Remember — that was the whole purpose of our arrangement, to discourage that sort of attention. It certainly did the trick last night. Worked like a dream.'

Roz stared at him, but his expression didn't change; he could have been carved from stone. A huge sob welled up in her throat, but she swallowed it with difficulty and a great determination, swearing to herself in that long, tormented minute after he stopped speaking that he would never, ever, know the vicious blow that his words had dealt her.

'You bastard.'

Her own voice was low, and it was quite steady, unlike the legs that somehow carried her through the door, and out into bright spring sunshine that mocked the grey misery in her heart.

She knew, with certainty, that she couldn't face Aunt Ellen, see her bright happiness, and keep her own wretchedness hidden. Her aunt knew her too well and would see through her in a minute. The truth, she knew, would have to be told — but not yet.

Roz crept to the front of the house like a thief in the night, and managed to make it inside and up the stairs without attracting the other woman's attention. Her own bedroom door had barely closed behind her when she gave way to a scalding torrent of tears that burst forth like a dam.

Curled like a wounded animal, she pulled the warmth of the quilt around limbs that were chilled and shaking as if with an ague, and cried until she could cry no more, and only then did she ask herself — *Why?*

Was she crying for the future that had been so carefully planned and now probably lay in ruins? For the career that had been held tantalizingly before her, like a golden ladder just waiting to be climbed, and might now have been moved out of her reach because of this adverse publicity? Was she crying for the man who was to have been a part of it all, and would now probably be only too glad that it wouldn't be his ring that she was wearing?

Roz stared up at the ceiling, her eyes wide and disbelieving, as she was forced to acknowledge with a sense of shock and dismay that none of it mattered that much after all. Those dreams and careful plans, the life in London that she had thought so right for her that she could live no other, were suddenly handfuls of dust — and just as easily disposed of with the minimum of hurt and regret.

What she really wanted — and had spent so many years denying — was everything that her aunt had always wanted for her; but the biggest shock of all, and the one that she had the most difficulty grasping, was that the man she wanted to share it all with — was Sam!

It was, she decided, like following a pinpoint of light along a dark tunnel, and then suddenly, blinking, you walked out into brilliant sunshine. For the first time you could see everything so clearly that it made you wonder why you had never seen it all before.

She loved him — loved Sam Lawrence, country and western singer, Sam. He was the man she was in love with, and probably had been for longer than she would have believed possible. Roz repeated it over and over again, feeling the words, tasting them, and enjoying the way they felt on her tongue.

She sat up straight on the bed, throwing the quilt to one side, letting a smile begin to bloom on her face as she acknowledged her own stupidity. Why hadn't she known? Why hadn't she realised that the attraction that had always been between them — an attraction she always carelessly dismissed as being no more than friendship — had been growing steadily into love? It had only needed the recent period of time spent in each other's company to drive them into each other's arms.

Laughing, she jumped up, impatient to go and find Sam — to tell him . . .

The laughter died, and without the smile her mouth drooped sadly. She had forgotten — how could she have — that though she might have discovered her love for Sam, it was a love that most definitely wasn't returned? He had been using her — had freely admitted as much. If she went to him now, if she offered him her newly-discovered love, there was no doubt in her mind that he would throw it, quite forcibly, back into her face.

Sinking back onto the bed, Roz found she could recall quite easily the look in Sam's tawny eyes each time he had kissed her. Funny, she mused, when she hadn't seemed to notice at the time. She remembered, too, how he had sung the words of the love song just as if he meant every single one, and she finally realised she felt the same way. Perhaps she would have recognised it sooner, if only she hadn't been so stubbornly certain that Sam wasn't what she wanted, and closed her mind to what was happening between them.

She was suddenly sure that he had known, and that he had wanted it, engineered it, even. But why, if he didn't really want her at all — was it all really just to keep the fans away?

He didn't have to make her fall in love with him, she told herself bitterly, and then she accepted with a sinking heart that he did it all the time. It was his job, purely and simply, as a singer of romantic songs, to make sure that his audience fell in love with him every time they watched him at a concert, and every time they played one of his records.

A professional heartbreaker, no less, and she had allowed herself to fall for a polished, perfectly-tuned performance — and the worst of it was that it was far too late for her to turn the clock back, even if she wanted to.

How long she sat there, staring into

space, Roz wasn't really sure. Her feelings ran the gamut of sorrow, anger, regret — and, quite often, longing found its insinuating way in.

*How can you still want him?* she asked herself. *He's made it abundantly clear that he used you to suit his own purposes, and yet you still hope, against all the odds, that he will suddenly confess that he returns your love.*

*Well* — She sat up straight, and pulled her shoulders back with grim determination. — *if he's waiting for me to fall sobbing at his feet, begging for crumbs of affection from his table, he'll surely have a hell of a long wait.*

All trace of grief was meticulously erased with the help of her usual make-up, and a generous application of concealer expertly applied beneath her eyes. Dressing in a bright cerise pink that clashed defiantly with her hair, she felt quite confident that no-one would know that beneath it all lay a broken heart.

Roz hadn't expected to have to face

Sam quite so soon, but as she approached the kitchen, the rumble of his deep voice announced his presence, and caused her to halt for a moment in her tracks. Almost immediately, she forced her reluctant feet to move forward, telling herself sternly that this was no time to be faint-hearted.

Something was wrong. She sensed it, even as she put a trainer-clad foot over the threshold, and one look at her great-aunt's stricken face confirmed it.

She looked to Sam for the reason, and there she found it. She knew what it was before he even opened his mouth to explain, in a hard tone full of the dislike for her that she could see so clearly written in his eyes. 'I've told Ellen that, to our regret, we have decided that it would be prudent to end our engagement. Despite the evidence to the contrary, marriage is no longer what either of us wants, and *that* — ' He flicked a dismissive finger towards the cuttings on the table. ' — was no more than a farewell kiss.'

He sounded so pompous, and so unlike Sam, that she found herself staring at him in amazement. It sounded just like a statement to the press — but of course, she reminded herself, that was just what it would eventually become.

How could he? Without taking the time to discuss the wisdom of making such a move, without even waiting for her presence to try and soften the blow, he had once more, gone his own sweet way, with no thought for the consequences that he had urged her to consider such a short time ago.

She bit back the angry retort that so desperately needed to be said, and without so much as another glance in his direction, she turned all of her attention to Aunt Ellen.

'I'm so sorry.' She wrapped her arms tightly around the older woman's frail body, and she promised herself that if the shock should cause her aunt any harm, she, personally, would see that

Sam paid dearly for what he had done today.

'I must admit it's a bit of a blow.' Aunt Ellen sounded so unlike her usual self, as if she had had all the 'go' knocked out of her. 'So unexpected — after all that,' she indicated the newspaper cuttings still strewn across the table, 'which now, of course, you've explained.'

Roz looked over the frizzy white head at the black-and-white printed proof of her own foolishness. She should have one framed, she told herself harshly, as a permanent reminder to never again let her heart rule her head. Had it really only been just over a week ago that she had been planning a sensible and realistic future . . . ?

With a superhuman effort she forced her attention back to her aunt and, with a freezing glare in Sam's direction, said, 'You shouldn't have been told like that. It was cruel and unkind.'

She watched the dark flush climb up over his rigid jaw with a strong sense of satisfaction at having managed to hit him where it hurt, at last. What on earth had made him suddenly decide that the time was right, after all that he had said to her to the contrary? Roz had a horrible suspicion that he had actually begun to think that she, like the young girl at the hotel restaurant, was about to make a nuisance of herself, and that he wanted her out of his life before she did.

'However,' she went on, and there was no hesitation in her voice, 'Sam was right in that you did have to be told, and even if he could have been a little more — er, sensitive — about it . . . well, it's too late for regrets now. I, for one, have none. It was all a mistake from the start.'

The eyes that met hers over her aunt's head were as cold and hard as pebbles. All hint of the Sam she had known for seven long and friendly years seemed to have disappeared without a trace. Roz suppressed a shiver, and wondered if he had been a figment of her imagination all along.

'There's no reason for us not to remain friends,' Sam said suddenly, and her head came up as she stared at him in patent disbelief.

He wanted them to be *friends*? He could think of *no reason* that they shouldn't be? She bit back the angry retort that threatened to tumble from her lips, and instead she offered, for her aunt's benefit and to get her away from Sam's immediate vicinity, 'I'll put the kettle on. I think we all need a cup of tea.' *And one of us,* she added silently, *really needs to have it poured right over his good-looking head, to show him just what I think of his stupid suggestion.*

The thought, however childish, made Roz feel a whole lot better. She even managed a slight twist of her lips in appreciation as she watched the water gush into the kettle she was holding — only to drop it with a clatter into the sink when Sam appeared silently at her side and put a hand on her arm.

'Don't you dare touch me,' she

hissed, with such venom in her tone that his hand dropped immediately, and he took a good step back.

He recovered quickly, and offered, 'I thought we should try to get along — for Ellen's sake.' He kept his tone low and even, and despite all that had gone wrong, Roz wanted to cry out to him, to plead, *What about our sake, Sam? What about that?*

Instead, she flashed him a brilliant and totally false smile, and agreed. 'Of course — for Aunt Ellen's sake.'

Roz looked in her aunt's direction quickly, concerned that she might have overheard their heated exchange, and she caught the older woman looking at them in such a strange — almost knowing — way. In a minute, it was gone, and she wondered if she had imagined it; and, if not, what it meant. Then, she shrugged and busied herself setting the cups out on the tray.

'Extra sugar for you,' Roz ordered, with affected cheerfulness in her hearty tone. 'I know the abrupt end of our engagement has been a shock to you after so long, but it really is for the best.'

'Oh, yes.' Aunt Ellen took the cup with a surprisingly steady hand. 'I'm sure that it is.'

She sounded so untroubled that Roz stared at her, and then found Sam doing the same with a mystified look in his eyes, until, with a shrug, he reached for his own cup and turned away. They had obviously been worrying about nothing where Aunt Ellen's feelings were concerned.

It was a struggle to keep any sort of conversation going, and the chiming of the doorbell was a welcome interruption in Roz's opinion. She jumped up almost merrily to answer it, offering, 'I'll get it.'

'Front door,' her aunt indicated, 'probably that late guest, so show him into the front room while I fetch my Visitors' Book.'

Relief at her escape from an atmosphere that could be cut into thick slices made Roz pin an extra-wide smile on her face. Whoever it was, she told herself, would be a more than welcome diversion from stone-faced Sam Lawrence, and she threw the door open with a theatrical flourish.

'Hello, Rosalind. Aren't you going to ask me in?'

To say she was speechless was an understatement; to say her jaw dropped could never have described the way it almost hit the carpeted floor as she stared in amazement at the fair man standing on the front step.

Only Aunt Ellen's, 'Who is it, dear?' finally put words into her open mouth, and gave her back the good manners that had momentarily deserted her.

'It's for me,' she returned in a shaky voice, and to the man, she said, 'Hello, Andrew. You'd better come inside.'

# 10

Roz found herself totally unnerved by the unexpected sight of Andrew Reynolds standing as large as life on her Aunt Ellen's front doorstep. For perhaps the first time in her life, she was quite unsure how to proceed.

She wanted to ask him why he had come, but she was very much afraid that she already knew the answer to that, and the question remained unspoken between them.

How odd it seemed when she realised that if Andrew had turned up only the day before, she would have been thrilled and delighted to see him. However, it was a long, long time since yesterday, she acknowledged, and too much water had flowed under too many bridges for anything to have remained the same.

Somehow, she found the sense from

somewhere to usher him into the front room, and to see him seated before she made her escape by insisting on bringing him tea that he was clearly going to have no interest in drinking.

Her relief at finding only Aunt Ellen in the kitchen was immense. She somehow knew that the two men were not going to get along at all, and the longer she could postpone the inevitable meeting, the better she would be pleased.

'A friend of yours, is it?' Aunt Ellen looked up from chopping onions. Her eyes were quite dry, and bright with curiosity.

'Yes,' Roz tried to sound enthusiastic, 'that's right, a friend — from London.'

'How nice.' The older woman smiled encouragingly. 'Why don't you bring him on through? Not very welcoming to leave him on his own, is it?'

Roz had a sudden cosy picture of Andrew drinking tea at the kitchen table, with Aunt Ellen chatting away and chopping onions right next to him. She shuddered, imagining the horrified look dawning slowly on his face as he became aware that the smell would be seeping steadily into the expensive fabric of his Armani suit.

'I'll take him some tea, have a chat, and then bring him in to meet you,' she promised, setting out her aunt's Poole Pottery china self-consciously, and trying not to notice the raised eyebrows as she did so. That particular china was only for royalty and the like, as far as Aunt Ellen was concerned — even her paying guests only had their meals and drinks served in the second-best china cups and saucers.

'There are sugar lumps in the cupboard.'

Roz looked at her aunt quickly, but could detect no sarcasm in her tone or her expression, though she knew that in the older woman's book, sugar lumps and the best china went hand in hand, so to speak.

'Andrew doesn't take sugar,' she said evenly, and — feeling totally embarrassed, no matter how much she told herself that there was no need — began to slice a lemon.

*Not everyone prefers their tea strong, liberally milked and sugared, from cheap and cheerful china,* she told herself, as she carried the tray through to the front room and set it down carefully on an occasional table. Her efforts were all wasted, as she had known quite well that they would be. Andrew left the tea to go cold in the cup.

Across the tray of cooling tea they viewed one another for long silent moments. Roz had time to study minutely the man who she had so recently been determined was all she had ever wanted in a husband.

*Nothing but the best* was Andrew's motto, and it showed. From the top of his expensively-cut fair hair, to the tips of his glossy, hand-stitched shoes, his whole appearance shrieked *money.*

Roz had always been impressed with the way he looked, and she had gone to considerable effort — not to mention expense — to dress and behave with the good taste and decorum that would compliment him in the way he had always expected, and almost demanded, of her.

Today, she found that his appearance no longer stirred her to admiration, and the critical looks he directed at her own casual clothing — that once would have sent her running to change — affected her not at all. She was in Dorset and on holiday right now, as she didn't need to remind herself. She no longer felt the pressure upon her, as she did in London, to look like a fashion plate during the waking hours of the day.

The silence lengthened between them, as Andrew waited with growing impatience, for Roz to speak first. She found that she was equally determined to let him begin, just to see what his reaction had been to a tabloid bomb being dropped into his carefully-laid plans.

She watched him carefully school his thin features into what he obviously, and probably very fondly, believed was a reasonable expression. He looked, she thought, much as he did when he was expecting unfavourable news from the stock exchange.

'I think,' he said ponderously, 'that you owe me an explanation,' he withdrew a creased copy of an all-too-familiar newspaper from the large envelope he had been carrying, and spread it with a look of distaste on the table beside the cooling tea, 'about this.'

'I know that I do.' Roz suddenly felt very sorry for him. 'And I sincerely apologise for the embarrassment that it must have caused you.'

'I simply can't — ' He tapped the front-page photo. ' — believe that you would ever behave in such a way, and in such a brazen fashion, that the gutter press could create this sort of a scandal out of it. Did you give no thought at all to what *this* — ' He tapped the page again. ' — would do to me, should it get out in the media that you and I are also involved?'

Andrew's pale city skin was flushed with annoyance, and Roz was suddenly quite sure that only his pride was hurt.

'Is it the fact that I was kissing another man that most upsets you?' she asked evenly. 'Or the fact that I made the front page while I was doing it?'

He had the grace to look a little uncomfortable and, she noticed, he couldn't quite meet her steady gaze. Roz was beginning to feel as if the scales were dropping from her eyes with monotonous regularity, and she wondered why the truth hadn't always been so readily available to her.

'Well, of course,' he blustered, 'I wasn't too happy about seeing my future wife in the arms of another man, but I quite realise that it must have been a moment of madness on your part. A *country and western singer* —' His tone couldn't have been more disparaging if he had tried. ' — is hardly your style, now is it, darling?'

He made it sound as if Sam's not-inconsiderable talent was worth slightly less than the ability to unblock a sink, and Roz felt her hackles rise immediately as she plunged in to defend him.

'Sam happens,' she informed him icily, 'to be fast becoming one of the top singers in his field, both here and in America, writing and performing all his own music. And,' she added, as if it clinched the matter — and it probably did where she was concerned, 'he happens to be a very good friend of mine, and has been for a number of years.'

Roz didn't even notice that Sam had been promoted from the role of the bad guy in her life, or that Andrew was rapidly putting himself in that unfortunate position.

'Friends?' Andrew pursed his lips. 'Yes, I see. So where, then, did these — these — Fleet Street hacks get the impression that you are in a — and I quote — 'a *long-term relationship* with the man?'

Roz felt heat burn her face like fire,

and she quickly hid the hand with the ring on it behind her back. She knew that he had her fairly and squarely there. She was definitely in the wrong, and for all that she wanted to argue in the face of his very obvious disapproval, she knew that she really had no defence against his righteous — and very reasonable, in the circumstances — accusations.

She had only just opened her mouth to begin a very lengthy and complicated explanation when, to her overwhelming relief, her aunt put her frizzy white head round the door, and complained bitterly, 'It's really too bad of you, Rosalind, to keep your friend shut away in here and not have the good manners to introduce him.'

'I'm so sorry!' She leapt to her feet, and hugged her aunt gratefully. 'How rude of me. This,' she indicated the scowling young man, 'is Andrew Reynolds, a colleague of mine from London. We work for the same firm, you know. Andrew, this is my great-aunt

Ellen. You've heard me mention her often.'

Roz was depending on Andrew's inbred civility, and to her relief he didn't let her down. Rising to his feet, he proffered a well-manicured hand, and said, with the politest smile she could have hoped for, 'How do you do — er, Miss . . . ?'

'It's Mrs, but call me Ellen, dear,' her aunt encouraged, looking suitably impressed at the immaculate appearance of the unexpected visitor, 'everybody does. Ah — ' She caught sight of the newspaper on the table. ' — I see you've seen the pictures, then. I thought they were very good, myself, but,' she shrugged her bony shoulders, 'I seem to be the only one. Now, tell me, what exactly do you do in the City?'

She settled herself comfortably on the sofa, and patted the seat beside her encouragingly. Andrew sat, looking so totally bemused and bewildered that Roz had to hide a grin. She'd have been willing to bet that Andrew had never met anyone like Aunt Ellen in his life before.

'I'll wash up these tea things,' she offered, and fled, grinning widely, to the kitchen.

*Well*, she admonished herself minutes later, as she leisurely washed the precious china in a bowl of warm water, *I don't know what you think is so funny. Not only did you choose the wrong man in the first place, but you've made it very certain that neither one of the two will want anything to do with you ever again — or any other decent man, come to that.*

She wondered how long Andrew would stay — probably as short a time as it took to listen to her explanation, and to tell her that he wouldn't want to marry her now if she paid him to, if she was any judge. She found herself pondering on why the thought troubled her so little when only a short time ago she would have been devastated.

The answer was there in the photos. She stood at the kitchen table staring down at the neatly-cut-out squares. It was there written all over her face: her love for Sam shone out even in such poor-quality pictures, and she was amazed that no-one else seemed to have seen it.

She shivered, wrapping her arms around her body; and, hugging herself tightly, asked herself if Sam really hated her as much as he professed to. Could he have kissed her like that, if he didn't feel anything for her? She was very much afraid that the answer was yes, and that in his line of work he had probably kissed hundreds of women who meant nothing at all to him, just to keep their loyalty so that they would keep right on buying his CDs.

Her life was a mess, and there was no way she could deny it. She found that she didn't really want to. It would have been far worse, she reminded herself, if she had married Andrew and then discovered, too late, that it was a mistake and he wasn't what she wanted at all.

She sighed heavily and then straightened her back. Best to deal with one thing at a time, just as her aunt had always taught her; and Andrew was sitting there in all his City glory, just waiting to be dealt with, so she'd better get it over with.

But Aunt Ellen, it seemed, had other ideas, and appeared determined to keep Andrew all to herself. She was chatting nineteen to the dozen when Roz went back into the sitting room, and to her amazement, Andrew was talking just as enthusiastically back.

Listening to him bragging — in a very well-bred way — about all that he had achieved in his life and all that he hoped to accomplish in the future, Roz found herself feeling very far removed from the hopes and ambitions he was setting out. It all suddenly sounded so coldly clinical, as if the people around him were nothing more than pawns in a game of life that was carefully mapped out, day by day, and year by weary year. She could finally accept, without surprise, that she would have been one of those pawns.

She couldn't understand why it had taken her so long to see that all their careful plans had been made in completely cold blood. Love had barely come into it — scarcely even been given a mention — it had all been convenience, career moves, and a carefully-laid programme, just as Sam had once so sensibly said.

That was how their whole life together would have been. Roz could see it clearly for herself, now. A detailed plot full of projected targets leading to the desired promotions and material possessions, that didn't include all the things that made life worth living, a life that had no room to spare for laughter, sheer enjoyment or for love.

She looked at Andrew with new eyes as she accepted that the reason there had been nothing between them but the most perfunctory lovemaking had nothing to do with respect, and everything to do with sex having no real place in his scheme of things. He got his thrills from success and recognition in the world of commerce, of that there was no doubt in Roz's mind, and she could never have competed with that.

Oh, probably after they were married he would have found her a weekly slot, somewhere between the other tedious but necessary things in life, like paying the bills and shopping for food. Andrew, she finally realised, knew nothing at all about being spontaneous, and that was probably what horrified him most of all about what he would see as her extraordinary behaviour.

'That's settled, then.' Aunt Ellen clapped her hands enthusiastically, breaking into Roz's revealing thoughts and making her jump into the bargain.

'What is?' She was almost afraid to ask.

'Andrew is staying with us until tomorrow.' Her aunt looked at her as if she were offering her a prize. 'Isn't that lovely? No point in him driving back all that way tonight, and luckily he has an overnight bag in the car.'

*Ready for any eventuality*, Roz thought wryly, knowing that Andrew wouldn't be seen dead in the same clothes two days running, not even in a small town in the county that he professed to despise.

'I'll just check on the evening meal.' Aunt Ellen rose with an agility that belied her years. 'You'll join us, of course, Andrew, as our very welcome guest?' she invited warmly as she left the room, and smiled at his nod of acceptance.

'You told me you had meetings all the week,' Roz didn't hesitate to remind him accusingly, not at all sure that she wanted him to stay now that he had made the effort to come.

'LB phoned me — this morning, on a *Sunday*,' Andrew was obviously eager to convey the seriousness of the situation, 'the minute someone told him the news. He told me to take the time needed to sort things out,' he added confidently. 'He even shuffled my commitments and moved a couple of meetings. He was quite confident that I could keep my name, and that of the firm, out of the papers. After all, in our circles yours is a name that few would recognise, and our personal attachment — yours and mine — thankfully hadn't yet become public knowledge.'

And now nor would it. Roz accepted this truth with little more than a feeling of relief. She wrinkled her nose in disgust. It was pretty obvious that Andrew had turned up here only to make quite sure that she didn't run to the papers to set the record straight and tell them that he was the one she intended to marry, after all. It had nothing to do with him fearing that he might be losing her to another, better, man.

That was the moment, and Roz was very well aware of it, that any tiny particle of feeling or respect that she might have had left for Andrew finally, and quite painlessly, died. He hadn't even asked for her side of the story.

She didn't have to imagine what Sam would have done in similar circumstances, because she was quite sure that he would have come steaming into the picture in his battered old cowboy hat with all his guns metaphorically blazing. He wouldn't let the girl he loved go, she was certain of that, without putting up the most spectacular fight to keep her in his own arms at whatever the cost to his career.

A lump of cold, hard pain settled in the region of her heart as Roz was forced to acknowledge that a love such as that would never be hers. If there had ever been the slightest chance that Sam might have come to love her, she had killed it, quite thoroughly, by her recent treatment of him — not to mention her indifference over the years.

Feeling more unhappy than she had ever been in her life before, she said flatly, 'Come with me, Andrew, and I'll show you to your room.'

★　★　★

Roz hid in her room until she knew that it would be dinnertime, and that if she delayed any longer, Aunt Ellen was not above sending Sam to come and fetch her.

She had made an extra effort with her appearance, not out of any kind of wish to impress anyone, but because it was the best way she knew of giving herself some much-needed confidence.

She wore a bright golden-yellow knitted dress that followed the contours of her slim figure with flattering and eye-catching accuracy. Her make-up she knew to be flawless, and the carelessly-ruffled hairstyle had taken a great deal of her time to achieve.

Everyone was sitting at the kitchen table, quite clearly waiting for her to put in an appearance before starting on the delicious roast pork that Aunt Ellen produced, without comment, as soon as she was seated.

Roz had expected it to be an uncomfortable meal, but in the event,

she should have been pleasantly surprised, as everyone was obviously
making a great effort to be very civil.
This actually had the unusual effect of
making her feel more on edge than she
had been previously.

She tried hard not to notice that
Andrew was, quite clearly, looking
down his long nose at Aunt Ellen's
home-cooked meal of succulent meat,
cooked to perfection, crisp roast potatoes, a variety of steamed vegetables,
and a jug of her signature thick, dark
gravy. He was not at all comfortable in
the cosy atmosphere of the big homey
kitchen, either, and she knew that he
would probably have been more at ease
sitting in isolated splendour in the
guests' dining room.

Watching him, it made her wonder,
all the more, how she had ever thought
for a minute that he would fit in to her
life away from London. Though she had
to admit that her great-aunt seemed to
like him, and her artless chatter more
than made up for any silences left by

the rest of them.

Roz wondered idly if Sam had known of Andrew's arrival before he dressed for dinner, because if so, he certainly hadn't made any concession with his dress. Wearing, as he was, faded but clean denim jeans, and a boldly-striped blue shirt, he looked relaxed in the extreme, and very attractive.

'Tell us all about your job, and those marvellous career prospects,' her aunt pleaded. 'It all sounds wonderful to me, and I'm sure that Sam is very interested, as he has business pursuits of his own.'

Sam looked anything *but* interested to Roz, though at least he made the effort to appear so, which was more than could be said for Andrew when anyone else offered anything to the conversation. It was easy to see — belatedly — that he was totally self-obsessed, and not just very confident in his own skin, as she had always fondly imagined.

Looking at the two men together, the

contrast was enormous, and not only in their looks, though the one was so slight and fair, and the other so tall, broad and dark.

Sam could probably have bought and sold Andrew, over and over, but no-one would have thought it to look at them. Money and appearance had never mattered much to Sam, she realised admiringly, and she was certain that he gave a great portion of his earnings to charity, though she could never get him to admit it.

*Look at the way,* she reminded herself, *that Sam drove Ellen's beat-up old estate car about town without a qualm or a thought for his image, while Andrew wouldn't be seen in anything less than a top-of-the-range Audi. And I bet he doesn't even own a pair of jeans,* she added inconsequentially.

The evening dragged on, with Aunt Ellen chirping like an encouraging sparrow, and making sure that Andrew remained centre stage, even as they moved from kitchen to sitting room.

Roz didn't know how Sam could stand it. She was having severe difficulty staying put herself, and wondered more than once why he didn't just excuse himself and make himself scarce. *At least* he *could*, she told herself bitterly, lending one ear to yet another of Andrew's tedious yarns.

At last Aunt Ellen yawned hugely, and told the room in general and Andrew in particular that she needed her beauty sleep and would be off to her bed.

'Well, I'll bid you goodnight, then.' Andrew smiled his best company smile, and added, heavy-handedly, 'Though I assure you that you are quite beautiful enough for someone of your age.'

Talk about a back-handed compliment! Roz almost snorted, and she knew that under any other circumstances she would have caught Sam's gaze and shared a sick grimace.

Ellen had barely closed the door behind her when the charming look and practiced smile was wiped from

Andrew's good-looking face. He stood up and turned on the pair of them with a comical scowl that he might have fondly and mistakenly believed was forbidding.

'Between the two of you,' he declared, having risen to his feet and drawn himself to his full height, 'you've done your best to make me into a laughing stock in the City. I just hope you are proud of yourselves.

That he looked ridiculous was Roz's first thought, because Sam absolutely towered over him. Her second thought was to wonder fleetingly if he had any real intention of turning this into a fight. She hoped not, because she was sure that Sam would win any confrontation with very little effort, and without taking his hands from the pockets of his denim jeans.

'You can leave Sam out of this,' she advised. 'It's me who owes you an apology for not being honest with you from the start. If I had been, none of this would have happened.'

'No,' Sam interrupted firmly, 'It was my fault for not doing as you asked immediately, Roz, and I apologise to you unreservedly — ' He turned to Andrew. ' — and to you for any embarrassment I've caused you. I wouldn't blame you if you wanted to put one right on my jaw. I know it's what I would feel like doing in the circumstances.'

There was a startled silence following this unexpected statement; and, unmoving, the two men looked from one to the other, as if taking stock.

'I don't think it need come to that.' Andrew came to his senses first, hastily making sure that there would be no chance of violence — which was to his credit, Roz supposed. 'I'm sure we can discuss this like rational human beings.'

'If that's what you want.' Sam shrugged. 'Perhaps you have some suggestions as to the best way to handle this, er — Andrew — because I must confess I'm at a complete loss myself.'

Roz looked from one to the other of

them, and without waiting for Andrew to reply, she told them, 'There's only one thing we — I — can do, and that is to make a statement to say that my engagement to Sam is at an end. As we both know, Sam, it was never real anyway. I can simply say that we grew apart, as we agreed.'

Andrew stared at her, his face flushed, as he said in a horrified tone, 'You weren't thinking of telling them that you and I . . . ?'

God, he was pitiful in his complete desperation to keep his own name and involvement out of the papers. Though Roz supposed that, in all fairness, she couldn't really blame him. Still, if she hadn't already come to her senses as far as he was concerned, she somehow knew that she would have been more than a little disappointed by his attitude.

'You needn't worry,' she assured him, with a touch of sarcasm in her even tone. 'I will be sure to keep any mention of you out of my announcement.'

She could feel Sam's curious gaze on her face, but she carefully ignored him, keeping her attention on the now almost-fawning Andrew, sickeningly grateful for what he must see as her reasonable stance in a very worrying matter.

'I think that would be wise.' He was back to being his charming best. 'And, of course, eventually, when this has all blown over, maybe . . .'

The insinuation was that they might eventually be able to pick up where they had left off, and it had obviously been offered as a pawn to keep her sweet. He was undoubtedly arrogant enough to assume that she would still want to be with him. Roz didn't bother to put him right; she felt that it really wasn't worth the effort.

'You seem to be forgetting one thing,' Sam drawled, looking from one to the other of them as if he didn't understand them at all, and had absolutely no intention of trying. 'When you tell the press that we have grown apart — how are you going to explain away that kiss?' He indicated the front page of the paper, still spread accusingly between them. 'It doesn't exactly give that impression, does it? And they are sure as hell going to take a lot of convincing that it meant nothing.'

'I think I'll leave you two to sort this out.' Andrew — *sidled*, Roz decided was the word — to the door. 'I'm sure between you, you'll decide what's best.' And then he was gone.

Sam stared at the door as it closed softly behind him, and then turning back to Roz, he said in a tone of deep disgust, 'And that's the guy you want to spend the rest of your life with is it?'

Roz didn't bother to confirm or deny it, because she knew that there was no point. What could she say? That she had fallen out of love with Andrew days ago? That was, if she'd ever been in love with him in the first place, which she now strongly doubted. Should she tell Sam that she was actually crazy about *him*, and then watch the horrified look that would dawn on his face?

Ignoring the question, she told him instead, 'I shall tell the papers that it was obviously taken from an angle and looks more than it actually was — that it was simply a farewell kiss. An *engaging* farewell, if you like.'

She didn't need to look at the photo again to know that the reporters weren't going to believe her for a minute, but as long as Sam did, she felt that somehow she would manage to get through this ordeal.

'We could leave it all for a while longer,' Sam suggested, 'until all the fuss has died down again. It makes no difference to me.'

*No*, she admitted silently, *and that's the trouble*. Aloud, she said, 'There's really no point, is there, Sam?' And, with her heart breaking slowly and painfully as she looked into his handsome and dearly-loved face, she added quietly, 'For us, it really is over.'

# 11

In the morning, it was all still there, despite all Roz had hoped, and her dreams to the contrary. The two men in — or, more accurately, out of — her life still had to be faced. And so, she reminded herself, with a firmness she didn't feel, did the press.

When she finally, and very reluctantly, plucked up the courage to creep downstairs, it was to find that Andrew had, without a by-your-leave, taken his place in the dining room for a breakfast he obviously expected to have served to him along with the handful of other guests.

Roz was so embarrassed by his behaviour that she could hardly meet Aunt Ellen's eyes, and without a word she served him herself, slapping his food down in front of him with unnecessary, but very satisfying, force.

'I never realised he could be so — so . . .' She fumbled for an explanation.

'Snobbish, rude, ill-mannered, impertinent, impolite, boorish . . . ' She looked up to find that Sam had taken over from her aunt, and was expertly snatching toast from the toaster with one hand while replacing the bread with the other. 'Take your pick, because they all describe him very accurately. The man is without a doubt a complete idiot, and the shame is that he doesn't realise it.'

Roz flushed hotly, and could find nothing to say in Andrew's defence. She didn't try very hard, feeling as she did that he didn't deserve loyalty from her when he had made no effort to give it himself.

'He's not used to our ways, that's all,' said a mild voice.

Trust her aunt to look for the best, even in someone like Andrew. Roz threw her a grateful glance, doing her best to ignore a derisive snort from Sam.

'I'm not very hungry this morning,' she told the room in general, and her aunt in particular, 'so I'll make a start on the beds, shall I?'

She was almost through the door before the reply came. 'If you like, dear.'

She worked steadily and with the ease of familiarity, glad to be doing something to help her aunt. It was as she was dumping yet another load of sheets into the huge linen basket that a movement down the hall caught her eye. She stopped what she was doing, and stood back in the doorway of the room she was working from.

She found herself staring in patent disbelief as Andrew tiptoed from his room and crept silently towards the stairs. He was so obviously intent on getting away without having to face any of them that for a moment Roz stood frozen to the spot, amazed that anyone could be so . . . She shook her head as words failed her.

He had disappeared from sight

before she was suddenly galvanized into action, and she sped, equally silently, after him. She caught up with him just as his hand reached for the Audi's door catch.

'Not going without saying goodbye, surely, Andrew?' she said acidly, taking great pleasure in watching him almost jump out of his skin. 'How very discourteous of you.'

'I was, of course, going to . . . ' he blustered.

'No, you weren't.' She smiled pleasantly. 'And I shall now take the trouble to tell you what a disgusting little — little *twerp* I've finally realised you are, and that I wouldn't marry you if you were the last *man* — and I use the term loosely — in the whole world. Oh, please — ' She put her hand up when it looked as if he might interrupt. ' — don't say another word — the hole you've dug yourself into since you arrived is quite deep enough.'

Andrew was flushed, and then went pale. He was, for once, speechless, and of the fleeting emotions to slide momentarily across his face, the clearest one was of relief. It didn't even hurt, Roz found, to know that he was so keen to be rid of her.

'Before you go . . . ' She kept the smile firmly in place. ' . . . there's the matter of the bed, breakfast, and the evening meal that you *enjoyed*,' she emphasised the word sarcastically, 'in my aunt's establishment. I think — ' She named a sum that made his fair eyebrows nearly disappear up into his hairline. ' — should just about cover it.'

He paid up without a murmur. Hiding a grin, Roz drawled, 'What? No tip for the excellent service we offered? Oh, well, never mind. We hope you enjoyed your stay, sir. Do come again.'

He drove off with unflattering haste, and, still smiling, Roz went back to her bed-making with a lighter heart. She wished that all her problems could be solved so easily.

'Was that Andrew I heard leaving?' Aunt Ellen came into the room carrying more fresh linen. 'I suppose he wanted to make an early start.'

'Something like that,' Roz agreed; and, passing over the wad of notes, told her aunt with a straight face, 'And he insisted on leaving you this. He really enjoyed his stay with us.'

Aunt Ellen looked at the money, and she looked very hard at her great-niece, but refrained from comment, which wasn't a bit like her. Roz wondered, fleetingly, if she knew more than she was letting on; but she too refrained from asking.

They worked together in silence for a while, but Roz didn't miss the worried glances that were coming her way all too frequently, and so she was quite ready for the question when it came.

'What are you going to do? You and Sam?'

'Us? Oh, don't worry about us, we'll just go our own sweet ways,' Roz kept her tone deliberately light, and tried hard to ignore the searing pain that saying it caused her, 'which we've pretty

211

much always done anyway.'

'Are you sure that's what you want?'

*No*, she wanted to scream. *That's not what I want. It's not what I want at all. I want him to realise that he loves me the way that I love him, so desperately that it hurts, but I think we both know that it will never happen.*

Aloud, she said, 'What I want, is to get back to normality again.' She sat beside her aunt on the unmade bed. 'I wish I could tell you that I could be happy living here with you, but I really can't stay. It would be impossible for me.'

Actually, it wouldn't be impossible to live with her aunt now that London had suddenly lost its appeal. What *would* be impossible would be Sam arriving on the doorstep whenever he could get home, and having the heartbreak of seeing him eventually settle down with someone else. Oh, no, that would be much more than she could bear.

Her aunt didn't argue, but Ellen didn't fool Roz with her calm attitude, because she knew that, between them, she and Sam had hurt the elderly lady deeply by their deceit, and she regretted it with all of her heart.

Lunch was eaten almost in silence, with each of them seemingly lost in thought. Roz pushed her food listlessly around her plate but, looking up to find Sam watching her, she forced down a mouthful of pie that she definitely didn't want at all.

Aunt Ellen reached out for the teapot, offering, 'More tea, anyone?' Roz was horrified to notice that her hand was shaking, and a quick glance at her face told her that her aunt was a little paler than was usual, too.

'Are you feeling quite all right, Ellen?' Sam must have noticed, because he asked the question before Roz got the chance.

'I do have a tiny bit of a headache,' she admitted reluctantly. 'I might go and have a little lie-down — if I could leave you both to clear up for me, that is?'

'Of course,' they answered unanimously, and Roz promised, 'I'll bring you up a cup of tea at about three o'clock.'

'Thank you, dear. Thank you both for your concern, I shall be all right presently.'

'We've upset her,' Roz said sadly as the door closed behind her.

'I know,' Sam agreed, 'and I'm beginning to wish that we could turn the clock back.'

Back to before they had entered into the phoney engagement was what he meant, she knew. Roz glanced at the pretty ring, still firmly in place on her third finger as it always was when she came home to Brankstone, and found that she couldn't, in spite of everything, wish the same. She could only wish, fruitlessly she knew, that she could turn the clock on and make everything turn out very differently for them in the future.

'Do you really intend to tell the papers that it's over?'

In answer, she slipped the ring slowly and with great finality from her finger and, holding it out to him in the palm of her hand, she said, 'I think that's best, don't you?'

Silence hung between them, and Roz found that she was holding her breath; hoping, praying, that he would deny it, and beg her to change her mind about what she was so set on doing. Of course, that didn't happen.

He accepted the ring without glancing at it, and slid it into his pocket. His steady gaze never left her face as he said, 'I expect you're right.'

'Should I phone them?'

She didn't have to tell him that she had no idea how to go about speaking to the media, and she looked to him still to guide her.

'Leave it to me, and I'll arrange a meeting with the press. Or, better yet — ' He seemed to hesitate and then come to a decision. ' — since I intend to be there beside you if you insist on going ahead with this, I could approach

215

Solent Radio about extending the forthcoming interview slot to include us both. I'm pretty sure we can trust them to handle our story in a fair and sensitive manner — and allow us to at least have our say — unlike the tabloid hacks who will go out of their way to embroider and embellish every word to sell papers. Yes.' Sam nodded. 'I think that will be for the best if I can pull it off.'

'Thank you.'

'Will you go back to London, when it's over? You'll probably come in for a bit of attention for a while.'

'I don't intend to hide.' Roz lifted her chin proudly.

Sam smiled, and her heart turned a crazy flip-flop that was a strange mixture of love and grief.

'I didn't think you would for a moment,' he assured her, 'but how will Andrew cope with that sort of pressure?'

He was very careful to keep any hint of criticism from his tone, having previously had his say, and she wondered again why it had taken her so long to realise just what a special man Sam was.

'He won't be under any pressure,' she said flatly, 'because he won't be part of my life, and the press won't be aware that he ever was if I can help it.'

He looked at her strangely. 'Until all this has blown over, you mean?'

'No, that's not what I mean. He has no place in my life, and I wonder now why I ever thought that he did.' Roz managed a wry grimace.

A grin tugged at the corners of Sam's mouth. 'A momentary lapse in your usual impeccable good taste, I guess,' he suggested drily. The next moment they were laughing uproariously, the tension between them dissolving, to Roz's infinite relief.

In the midst of the merriment, their glances suddenly and unexpectedly met, and held. Then they weren't laughing any more. In an instant the atmosphere changed until it was charged with an emotion, an awareness that was almost palpable. Neither of them moved, as if they were afraid that the spell would be too easily broken.

'Roz?'

There was a question in his hoarse tone, but try as she could — and she did try — Roz wasn't sure what it could be, and she could only stand and stare.

'Please tell me I'm not imagining . . . ' He swallowed deeply and finished. ' . . . whatever there is between us right now, because you feel it too, don't you?'

She couldn't answer for the lump that formed in her throat, and could hardly see him for the tears that misted her eyes. She could only hold out her arms in mute surrender.

All the pent-up longing of the past few days was there in the hands that reached around his neck, in the fingers that buried themselves in the rich, dark hair and drew his face down to her own.

'Sam . . . ' His name whispered past

her lips as she gave herself up to the magic of a kiss that left her shaken to the core of her being.

With a deep groan he gathered her tightly to him, and she knew, quite surely, that this time he would never let her go. In each other's arms they savoured a long moment of true understanding, and all without a word of explanation having as yet been spoken.

Sam lifted a tanned hand to ruffle the fiery red of her hair. 'I've known for so long that I love you, and that we could be special,' he murmured hoarsely, 'but I was beginning to think that we would never make it.'

'So was I,' she confessed; and then, staring up at him, 'What did you say?'

'I was beginning to think . . . '

'Before that.' She was out of his arms now, taking a determined step back. 'You said, 'I've known for so long that I love you'.' She shook her head, as if to clear it, 'But when did you know — and how? Why didn't you tell me?'

'Let me ask you a question first.' He cupped her chin with a firm hand. 'When did you know?'

She met his gaze steadily and nodded sadly before she admitted, 'It took me a lot longer, and I only knew for sure these last few days, but I do think I must have loved you for a long time before that and never admitted it — even to myself.'

'That's what I thought — hoped — when I talked you into the phoney engagement all that time ago. I was sure you felt something more than friendship for me, and I had hoped it might help to steer your thoughts in the right direction — my direction. I never dreamed it was going to take years for what was so obvious to me to sink into your pretty head.'

Roz was puzzled. 'Why didn't you just tell me?' It seemed so simple to her.

'And have you feel pressured by me, as well as by your great-aunt, into settling down before you were good and ready? You were so determined that a career in HR without the encumbrance of a family was exactly what you wanted. I felt pretty safe to allow you the time you needed, and then — ' He grimaced ruefully. ' — right out of the blue, you announced that you intended to end our engagement and marry someone else. Is that any way to reward my patience? I had to take drastic and immediate action.'

'So, you talked me into coming home, but — ' She was curious. ' — what if I had refused to come?'

Sam gave a growl, and pulled her back into his arms. 'The other plan was to come and get you — on a white charger, if that was what it would take to make you see me in the right way.'

She giggled and nuzzled his chin with her own. 'What a splash that would have made. I think I'd have liked that. I never could resist a hero.'

'And I really do like the sound of that. I might even use it for my next song — and, by the way . . . ' He paused and spoke seriously. ' . . . every single one was written with you in mind. Didn't you ever know that?'

Roz shook her head wordlessly, and so many things suddenly made a lot of sense to her.

'We can have it all, you know,' he promised softly, 'with a little give and take, and compromise, we can do it. I don't expect you to give everything you've worked for up for me.'

'We'll talk about it,' she promised, 'but somehow, I think some of my priorities may have changed just recently, and London seems to have lost its appeal. I'm sure I can further my career just as well here in Brankstone, and be here to support to Aunt Ellen the way that she's always supported me.' Grinning, Roz said, 'She is going to be so made up.' She held out her left hand. 'May I have my ring back now, before we make that tea and go and tell her?'

Sam slipped the ring from his own little finger, and placed it firmly back in place. The stern tone was softened by the smile on his face as he asked, 'Before we do, can we be *quite* clear that there is nothing the least bit *temporary* about this arrangement?'

Laughing, Roz dropped to one knee and asked, 'Perhaps you would like to marry me, Sam, and make this arrangement into a permanent one?'

'Now, why didn't I think of that,' he grinned, 'because there's nothing in this world I would like more.'

Roz knew that the look in his eyes was mirrored in her own as he lifted her to her feet and drew her into his arms. The certainty of knowing that tomorrow, and all the other tomorrows, were there in front of them for the taking, made her heart swell with a joy that, with Sam's kisses, took all of her remaining breath away.

'And about time, too,' said Aunt Ellen severely from the doorway. 'I was beginning to think the pair of you would *never* get your act together.'

We do hope that you have enjoyed reading this large print book.

Did you know that all of our titles are available for purchase?

We publish a wide range of high quality large print books including:
**Romances, Mysteries, Classics**
**General Fiction**
**Non Fiction and Westerns**

Special interest titles available in large print are:
**The Little Oxford Dictionary**
**Music Book, Song Book**
**Hymn Book, Service Book**

Also available from us courtesy of Oxford University Press:
**Young Readers' Dictionary**
**(large print edition)**
**Young Readers' Thesaurus**
**(large print edition)**

For further information or a free brochure, please contact us at:
**Ulverscroft Large Print Books Ltd.,**
**The Green, Bradgate Road, Anstey,**
**Leicester, LE7 7FU, England.**
**Tel:** (00 44) **0116 236 4325**
**Fax:** (00 44) **0116 234 0205**

# ENDLESS LOVE

## Angela Britnell

Twenty years ago Gemma Sommerby and Jack Watson shared a summer romance, but after he left Cornwall she never heard from him again. And now, large as life and twice as handsome, he's back ... Gemma can't afford to open her heart to him and risk being hurt again — and Jack is just as disconcerted to find she affects him as much as ever. Why did it really go wrong between them all those years ago? And could they still have a future together?

# THE EMERALD

## Fay Cunningham

Cassandra Moon knows her mother Dora has a special talent — but will it be enough to protect the eccentric older lady when she is abducted in the depths of winter? Once again, Cass finds herself teaming up with DI Noel Raven, whom she argues with and is attracted to in equal measures. But the only way she and Noel can save Dora is to accept the bond of love that joins them together, so they can harness the power of the emerald ring and bring down the evil Constantine . . .

# TROPICAL MADNESS

## Nora Fountain

Paediatrician Serena Blake's idea of adventure is applying for a new hospital job in Dorset. Then her brother introduces her to the ruggedly handsome journalist and adventurer Jake Andrews, and she finds herself agreeing to accompany him to the African jungle in order to help sick and injured children. Soon the pair find themselves in the middle of an impending coup. And to make matters worse, Serena discovers that she's falling in love with Jake, though she's sure he will forget about her once — and if — they get back home . . .